W9-DHV-487

# PROMISE
# OF DAWN

## Other Books by the Author

The Art of Peace — Balance Over Conflict —
Tarcher Putnam 2003

Be a Light unto Yourself — Andrews McMeel 2003

World's End — Tarcher Putnam 2003

History of the Future — Pocket Books 2002

The Illustrated Rumi — HarperCollins 2001

The Millennium Planner — Viking Studio Books 2000

Prayer — Language of the Soul — Rodale 1997

The Buddhist Directory — Tuttle Books 1997

Revelation — The Apocalypse and Beyond —
Simon & Schuster 1995

The Quotable Spirit — Macmillan 1996

Nostradamus — The Millennium and Beyond —
Simon & Schuster 1990

Wonderchild — Simon & Schuster 1989

Superstitions — The Ancient Lore — Simon & Schuster 1988

Ironhorse — Doubleday 1987

# PROMISE
# OF DAWN

A Novel of Love After Death
inspired by a True Story

*Philip Dunn*

*A Crossroad 8th Avenue Book*
The Crossroad Publishing Company
New York

The Crossroad Publishing Company
481 Eighth Avenue, New York, NY 10001

Copyright © 2003 by The Book Laboratory™ Inc.

All rights reserved. No part of this book may be reproduced,
stored in a retrieval system, or transmitted, in any form or by
any means, electronic, mechanical, photocopying, recording, or
otherwise, without the written permission of The Crossroad
Publishing Company.

Printed in the United States of America

This book is typeset in 12/16 Cochin.
The display font is Galliard.


**Library of Congress Cataloging-in-Publication Data**
Dunn, Philip, 1946-
  Promise of dawn : a novel of love after death inspired by
a true story / Philip Dunn.
    p.  cm.
  "A Crossroad 8th Avenue Book."
  ISBN 0-8245-2122-6 (hardcover)
  1. Death – Fiction.  2. Future life – Fiction.  I. Title.
PR6112.O75P76 2003
823'.92 – dc21

                                              2003011460

1  2  3  4  5  6  7  8  9  10        10  09  08  07  06  05  04  03

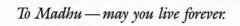

*To Madhu — may you live forever.*

*If I lie down one day and die in my sleep,*
*How will I know if I still dream,*
*A dream of death in life or a*
*Dream of life in death? That maybe I will wake again a*
*child*
*Still dreaming.*
*And how will I know which life I*
*Have left before sleep,*
*And which life I have come to*
*On waking?*
*Would I dream of dying*
*Or die of dreaming?*
*And is there a difference?*

# ONE

She comes always unexpectedly and never stays as long as I wish. We sit and talk or walk the beach and her thick black hair fades from the truth, in and out of the veil. We speak of the past, and the river of our lives together, and she asks me that question each time, always the same question, with the tone of one who has all the time in the world: "How is the kiss? Can you still feel it?" And I say always the same thing: "Yes, I still feel it."

A month after Nicki died, I was still in the same place, still living in Mill Valley, still working at UC Berkeley, still frightened of the same things. I had discovered that a life partner is a life partner until she dies, and then she becomes a saint. Everything I didn't like about her evaporated, and everything I did like became a hundredfold greater and more memorable.

My love affair was twelve years old when the woman who made everything possible lay back on her favorite pillow, and swallowed thirty carefully counted sleeping tablets with the help of a half glass of vodka, her eyes already glazed from the pain of the cancer, and her heart filled with the love we still shared.

Her body, when I returned from my day on campus, was exactly as it had been years before when we first met, when she was nineteen — tanned, young-breasted, dark-haired, and with that teenage-slimness. Such was her tender beauty that I didn't want the doctor to see her when he came to define her death, nor the police he called, who thought only in nightmares. We all knew that it was a crime to see such a woman as Nicki without her life intact, except that somehow her vitality remained etched in her face and body.

She wore her Victorian nightdress, bought years before in London — slightly flawed and gloriously decadent, wrapping the curves and floating the colors of her skin and hair. She was dressed for a passionate encounter — one that neither of us would ever fulfill. She had even made up her face and shampooed her hair, remarkably, given the pain she had suffered recently. There was a grotesqueness about it all, however, as though death hadn't yet arrived on the scene, as if we all stood there waiting for the event.

The utility room, next to the bathroom, was filled with neatly ironed and folded household linens — sheets, towels, shirts hanging. The spare bedroom was ready for guests, as though she thought I might need company after her departure. The kitchen was cleaned, her office filed and tidied — her projects in order. All this almost killed me as I imagined her moving about the house performing these last tasks without me, and we could not even talk about it when I returned, the way we talked always about everything. I could not hear from her about her last day or her death, and for weeks after I kept waking in the night wanting to ask her what had happened and tell her how I felt about it all.

I had asked her to die in my arms, after all — for me to share her death, and she had denied that. But I had asked many things of her in life which she could not grant, no more than any lover can. Her death had been her own as much as anything could be, for no doubt she did not want to hurt me with it — though hurt it did, nevertheless.

Vodka had worked well for her in recent weeks, calming her suffering, and in this last instance she knew she could not unswallow it, and so long as she didn't lose her courage, the body would do its work inevitably. And with this single complex act of insanity she changed the lives of all those around her.

For a week I dealt with the death retinue of California probate — police suspecting, lawyers objecting, relatives rejecting. Only I was left alone without definition. So I disappeared into the cubicles of my life — cooking voraciously for anyone who would eat, writing unnecessary tracts for work I cared nothing for, repairing and enhancing my pet classic car in the garage — anything to define, anything to reclaim the space of her absence. The kitchen hurt particularly but it provided solace — a bitter-sweetness that arose from her presence there. All that I knew about cooking had come from her patience and piquancy, for I had learned the essence of the dishes she taught. I loved to flavor, but most of all I loved to taste the wines that accompanied the results of my work. I was a cook by nature — should have been by trade — but never gave it my full concentration. She, on the other hand, was Spanish, and her culinary gifts left me and our guests utterly breathless.

I lost myself, those following days, in the overfilled qualities of my overfilled kitchen. I dwelled on my guests with sophisticated dishes, utterly simple Italian complexities that I served up before naïve American noses. The guests, old friends and new, indulged me willingly, leaving me free to die of my emotions.

With a sweating hob I created perfect pasta, supreme entrees, delectable deserts — vibrating between tears, carnivorous prayers, and champagne laced with sugar cubes and cognac to the puzzlement of my kitchen coterie — the soulful, careful gathering that my local community offered at the death of my loving wife.

Only the nights really wrecked me. Forever, alcohol cooked my mind and body against the dead, while some wild notion of postprandial peace attempted to close the shutters to death, while I slinked from my bed to find digestive represents. I replied to Nicki's postvital gestures by pursuing my own disorientation and regeneration — a life after death with a death after life.

I would be asleep by noon, with top-ups and regurgitations by four — the timing quite precise, coinciding with the schedule of my cats, who loved my hot skin on the bed for their afternoon naps. The result, of course, was nothing but depression. So I had to give it up — reluctantly. How could I continue? What was existence if it provided anomaly so eager in torture?

I burned Nicki's body in a Catholic crematorium and secretly uttered Hindu prayers, then took the ashes and spread a small portion of them over a part of the land behind the house while chanting from the Tibetan Bardo, keeping the rest — I didn't know why, but it seemed right.

I went to the south coast of England to visit my parents in the hope that they could duplicate the comforts of my childhood somehow, but they couldn't. My eighty-two-year-old mother hugged me, cooked bacon and eggs, baked scones, puffed up my childhood bed, but I could see it was too stressful for her. My ninety-year-old father simply cried all the time.

I talked with them a little about my childhood, and if anything this made matters worse. In that world of long-gone English summers we took the family vacation, which, annually, was supposed to do for the mind and body what tea and money did for the heart, spent in places of dim recognition, close by pebbled sands in overpopulated, beach-hut-ridden mazes of bodies and suntan oil, with sweaty working-class men darting among sand-flicked tea-flask-holding grandmothers. Each year my father would drive the roads to those buckety-beaches with gritted teeth and tense expressions, constantly losing his way to the chant of my mother's irritation. On arrival we would find the rented cottage bereft of human warmth and cutlery, the last occupants having left none and taken the other. The places smelled of stale seaweed and dust, so that mother's tasks were more demanding even than at home, cleaning before the vacation could start, and maintaining her vigil throughout the statutory two weeks (just long enough to make you think you've had a break, but not long enough for you to realize that you haven't).

Here was the English "seaside" for the middle-class of the 1950s — postwar freedom for postwar depression — and my childhood, of course. I both loved it and hated it — an isolated, over-sensitive child reaching for my teens, longing for adulthood. But these were but memories, and I could only walk the memory beaches for so long — life had to continue, after all, how could it do otherwise?

So I kissed them both and thanked them for their love, and went home again. As I left their front door my mother touched my face with those tender, puffy palms, and said: "Don't let it make you crazy." It had never occurred to me that she had such insight, but then I realized that this was natural — that she would think that I might go the way Nicki had gone, dive into the bottle and swallow the pills as she had. None of us knew at that point that the opposite was the truth.

I understood during those coming days after I left England and returned to the U.S. that I would only survive this condition — this deliberate death experience — if I took myself in hand. I had to be as absolute in life as she had been in death. But during the interminable flight back to San Francisco, I fell asleep and did not wake even when we landed. The stewardesses and the pilot who came to inspect my condition thought I was in a coma and, after vigorous attempts to wake me, called 911.

I welcomed the world taking over my body, and remained safely in San Francisco's best medical environment far longer than I should have. I undertook, during the postcoma recovery, to write that book I had been promising myself all those years on the subject of the paranormal, of course, and the way to deal with grief. All the pain and troubles of my own experience and my attempt to exorcise it went into that manuscript, with a subtle underscore of agony over the violence of a lover's suicide. I was writing about the grief brought about by the loss of the dearest lover, while beneath it all, my hand dipped into the river of hate and anger that I also felt for her. My boat displaced the Styx while I pretended to be beside the Ganges. The book itself, needless to say, got written only in my mind.

This irreversible condition lasted another week, and still my memories and doubts — my pain and self-pity — refused to reside in death with Nicki. I woke every night and began to understand that my mind and body actually relished this ritual of hurt. So it became time to stop. So I did one night, and it was that night that she returned.

He looked different, sprawled there on the morning bed, crumpled and innocent, no attitudes, no bound-aries. His hair fell awkwardly as though it might grow back into his head, unaware of the comb that would part and straighten. There was no respectabil-ity anywhere on his body, except for that of sleep. His slight, tender belly lay upon the ravaged sheets, his loosened genitals thoughtlessly abandoned. No woman would care to rouse him now — too many consequences. One broad arm grasped the pillow, claiming this the last lover. One leg took refuge, sheet-wrapped by a percale, untidy corset. The other nuzzled my pillow, my partnership, my ever-loving absence.

It hadn't occurred to me before death that after it I would be able to see him again. Perhaps somewhere in my darkest, most flighty dreams I might have considered some fairy-tale fantasy, but I was genuinely surprised that I found myself standing there in his room looking at him. All the feelings were still available — the guilt at walking away from him the way I had, the loss of his presence, the regret that maybe I could have chosen another route — a plethora of emotions that I had not imagined would be present in the spirit of the dead. But who was I to imagine anyway — what vessel does imagination inhabit?

But everyone was there around me, literally everyone — the relatives, the friends who had gone before, the thoughts from forever, the emotions that had resided in and around my body all my life, the memories, the experiences — all present even more after death than before, because somehow I had access to a thousand lives. For those who think it all ends at death and that some preposterous heaven or hell ensues, forget it. This notion appears farcical when you're there. Nothing changes. Everything you imagined in life, you will experience in death.

"What is this sensation?" I kept quite still, pretending to be unaware of Jennifer's question. She began to repeat it after what seemed too long a silence, but I spoke, still without turning my head or changing my expression.

"Just a feeling. No more than that. A sense that she's still with me somehow. I don't know." I turned to Jennifer — Nicki's life-long friend.

"Does it hurt you, this feeling?" She seemed to suggest her own uncertainty and sorrow, but this only acted to reject my response. I wasn't eager to let her into my grief. I couldn't figure out my own feelings beyond that of overwhelming sadness, let alone share them, even with someone Nicki and I had known for so long.

"I can't say, really." I must have looked to Jennifer as though I wanted to cry, and she knew I wouldn't wish her to witness that, so she turned away. The two of us gazed out the window at the university buildings, the people drifting by armed with their academy.

The sun shone warm and I found my eyes wandering over the thin patches of grass that insisted between the paving stones directly outside the window. The cherry trees were just beginning to unfold their sticky leaves, and their buds were fully formed, ready to pop on the limes. Birds darted everywhere, preparing for spring. A couple of kids had been left on the main lawn, picking daisies and making necklaces that they were intent on hanging about each other's necks. I noticed that everything seemed pretty much all right with nature except for the adults, who generally looked miserable.

Jennifer did not say too much more. She did not tell me then of her strange dream. She said nothing of the time when she saw Nicki standing before her, waving to her to stop and rest, or so it seemed. Nicki was dead, after all, dead if not gone.

The blinds let in early light, the stark sun rising with the earliest birdsong. I was in America. California still. I searched the familiar location, but sensing dates was difficult. Behind the blinded windows I could see the gorgeous Marin County hills thick with forests. California, where they greet you carelessly. I would dwell here in my own way and watch again like I used to. I would dwell upon his life. Would that he could dwell upon mine. Would that I had had but a fraction of the truths in life that I had discovered since passing through the veil.

Movement slipped through his body as I turned away from the morning. An orange cat entered the room — small-headed, insistent, with the slightest fear of waking the master-cat. Gideon slipped back to his coma. I knew him to sleep lightly, but this had apparently changed. An arm flapped against the cat, which jumped and then crept back, body low. Who was the animal, his youthful eagerness pestering the boss-cat at this hour? Gideon's cats looked upon him as another cat, seeking out the fur and soft skin, knowing the tender-loving-care, or rough justice, that would have been meted out to them by the real thing. Which cat knows man? Which feline squirm comprehends the heavy-footed, awesomely clumsy, insensitive human?

∾

"Anyway, I'm not sure I want to stop it. It feels kind of nice to have her around." I turned my gaze from the quadrangle to Jennifer as she tried again to help me.

"Maybe if you try seeing it all as — I don't know — as part of your work. Maybe you could look at it professionally. Might help you incorporate it, include it in your book." She walked on thin ice.

"Yes, perhaps." I paused again, thinking about how Jennifer looked right now. She was pretty, dark haired and blue-eyed, with that Native American beauty. She wore her "Berkeley frock," which disguised the roundness of her body, with a shawl over her shoulders tied at the side. Her long bushy hair was gathered with a rough piece of cloth near the bottom end, and she frequently pulled on it, tugging it around to the front where it fell across her chest. I liked her attention. I missed attention, especially from women. But I didn't want to do anything about it, include her or involve her — I'd known her too long for that, and she had been Nicki's best friend for what seemed the whole of their lives.

Her suggestion of making all this part of my work was a welcome one. This *was* my work, after all. I *was* involved in phenomenology, so I had no need to excuse myself for these weird sensations that Nicki was still with me. As though dissolved in the thick, almost crude pain of loss and grief there was also the constant sensation of a loved-one's presence. It was a dense liquid that engulfed me — syrupy and tenderizing, unrelenting. I went to sleep with it, dreamed of it, woke up with it, and in among it all were lucid dreams of Nicki's life, of her terrible pain, her anxiety at the face of death, her courage, and finally her abandonment. It felt a little as though I could not admit to the loss of a limb — like a soldier after the war whose leg has been amputated, and the ghostly limb refuses to depart. Nicki was my ghostly limb.

I woke sometimes, about three in the morning with visions of her dilapidated expressions shortly before she gave up the struggle. I saw the looks of endgame in her eyes, demanding nothing but killing me nevertheless. I felt the guilt of realizing that sometimes I just wanted her to go and leave me alone, give me grace from her agony, let me be free of the responsibility of another human being in such impossible circumstances. And then there was the wrenching, appalling pain of loss, even before loss had occurred — that loneliness and sense of abandonment. These were the feelings that remained now.

And still, beyond all this, was that other image that recurred — a dark image of ancient origin. This troubled me every time I dreamed, every time I closed my eyes. And the ancientness of it was also fearful. It was as though some distant picture was being shown to me without the frame about it — not exactly a warning of danger, but an image of another, darker nature that waited for me. I rationalized it as an effect of Nicki's death — somehow a kind of pall that had descended about my head and was most prevalent at night — the kind of feeling that comes in the early hours when the waking consciousness and the busy excuses of life fail to cover up those fears and doubts. I had a sense in these moments that I would be subjected to changes I could only worry about in the present, for they possessed no form.

Boss-cat-arm splat, cat so fast it missed. Tashy the orange Abyssinian came back for more, the eagerness to exit, cat-flap-locked, what else can a cat-fella do? Keep pestering. Boss-cat lifted his tousled head. "What do you want? Leave me alone." Tashy comprehended, settling down close enough to keep nuisance, far enough to avoid that heavy paw.

Gideon knew he would inevitably have to get out of bed, but lying there he could feel my presence, the smell, even, of my soft pajamas, the essence of my skin. It all remained absorbed in the pillow he insisted on using, cuddling, enwrapping every night — my pillow. He had changed the sheets and pillow cases after I died, wanting somehow to get rid of the experience of my death, but he had kept the old ones unwashed for two weeks in the laundry because they still smelled of the things he needed to smell, still smelling of my body, still reflecting the pictures of me before I began the process of dying. Then he had put just the one pillowcase back onto my pillow, and like some cartoon character, would not, could not let it go.

He lay there, thinking of Jennifer and her attempts to help him, her hints that she knew what it was like for him. Had she some understanding of it? She worked in his department, after all. She knew all the stories of the afterlife, ghosts, spirits, phenomena. Did she know something she wasn't telling? She'd talked with him as though interrogating him.

"I don't know Jennifer. If I look at it squarely this sense of her presence is believable but outrageous, and yet I feel tremendous uncertainty. If I admit to it, it's frightening. If I deny it, it grows stronger. The presence isn't only memory. There are memories all the time but they come from my mind *because* of the sense of presence. The presence itself is solid, unexpected, as though living independent of me. I don't control it or change it. It happens, just happens, everywhere, all the time. I tell you Jennifer, she's here, with me, right beside me."

"Maybe we should do a regression, do you think?" She still wanted to help him, but there was that nagging question, so she cloaked it as a professional interest. She leaned forward and pulled her hair across her shoulder, wrapping her fingers in it, feeling secure

at the thick darkness of it. She noticed him look at
her briefly, fleeting past the gesture. She wondered if
he missed a woman beside him?

"I guess," he said. "Maybe soon. Not yet. I tell you,
the sadness is palpable. I can almost wash my hands
in it. I don't want to make a fool of myself yet. Can it
wait? I know you want to help but let's wait awhile."
He looked at her this time, square in the eyes. She
smiled her full-lipped smile and felt her eyes water
slightly at his response. Nurse Jennifer — one of her
favorites. Did he know? Did he know that she had
seen us together? Had I seen her seeing us on that
day in Mill Valley? But my heart went out to Jennifer
and her loving nature.

"Of course — there's no hurry, only if it helps."

I swear he saw I was watching — this feline marker.
I swear the cat knew that I cared, watching over
his master each hour. Only Gideon failed to see the
truth, because for him I was still only an uncertain
presence without definition, his mind and heart
wishing my return, his love and charity never elevated
to awareness. If only he could see past the veil, so thin,
so transparent. No matter, this would come. How did
I know?

I stood cautiously at the windowsill. The light burst
through like nothing on earth, yet 'pon earth it was.
From my own dark-side, cool-side, I saw the sun rise
fruitfully, offering enlightenment where none lay in
the hearts of man or woman. I saw Gideon's gentle,

senseless abandon; sadness writ large upon every feature. His work was in doubt and only a defense now. His creativity unborn, whereas it had dominated his life, when mine was still unfinished, unworthy. I saw none of the dwellness of our coupling in the absence of my body. He could not stretch yet to the imagination so initiate to our new partnership.

The morning began. He rose from the doubtful depression of our once-past-sleep. He still lived there where I had been. Every morning of our love affair he had risen early and prepared breakfast. Every morning he had flopped down the banister, slippers coaxing those flannel feet to encounter the kitchen for fruit and Green tea, tray embellished love-nest early mealtime. Cranking up the mountain-morning he would bring me repast — my precious groan, willing to let me grouse the early hour — so tired, so tired was I this day — everyday. Here we would sit and discuss the night, the dreams, the expectations. Here, again and again I would forget my consciousness and curse the mistakes of life, when the joy of it lay as a bright sunshine upon the sheets before me. We had lived and loved together for twelve years, since I was a child of only eighteen. He had been my father, protector, lover, dirty old man for all that time. I had learned from him, hated and loved him, been unfaithful to him, escaped from him, climbed away from it all in some attempt to be "free" from him, and it had never worked, except at the departing of course, and not even then.

Now he stood before the windows also, so close to me that I could almost smell his skin, that musty, morning breeze of manhood — him blisslessly unaware. His eyes were gray. In joy they became a deep-sea blue, when worries were pitched across the valley away from his mind. Sadness and preoccupation turned him gray, while brief moments, maybe minutes, of joy brought him always alive. Now the grayness was intense, and I longed to tell him that I stood beside him still, but I had no voice for it unless he heard. The words just slipped away from me into that nether forest where falling trees are silent.

He stood for a moment in the earliest of sunlight, uncertain. The branches swayed outside — everything would be okay. He looked as though a part of him had gone overboard, abandoned ship in the light of a terrible storm, and was now lost at sea. His tall, broad body seemed eager only to drape itself over the windowsill and spill outside onto the deck like some Dali painting. How I longed to put out my hand, still so attached was I.

He yawned and stretched. Maybe my pity and sadness wasn't so apt after all. I felt a mixture of hope and resentment. Did I find his feelings worse than they were? It would be good if I did. I turned away from the window's late bright spring. The urges of the body took over his movements — he was a man for breakfasts still, some comfort this gave me.

As he left the room I watched the way it changed, the shadows of light and the animals — now there were two cats in occupation — the Abyssinian and one of the two ash-colored brothers, who had entered through the bathroom window. They nuzzled one another. I wondered if they missed me too. They tumbled over each other, amusing themselves in those shadows and bright dashes of light, testing the next moves for a run about the house.

Gideon was gone downstairs and stood now in the kitchen, following his old routine. He turned on the radio to NPR, " . . . the only broadcast worth listening to." He hated American TV, though a huge five-foot-wide monster occupied the living room. The time we'd spent there together he would curse the "anticulture" of America — no passion, no beauty except in nature, no eroticism, no sex except in dirty parlors, no eccentricity but the lack of it.

I found his thoughts and listened, my heart swelling at every slight change in his emotions. He thought about me, about my presence, and I felt the tenderness that moved him. He touched things in the kitchen and withdrew his hand as memories flooded his heart. I had cooked for him so many times, always played the housewife, though always denying it, for this was but a patch on the rest of me. My fastidiousness annoyed him sometimes, while his clumsy untidiness had taken me years to accept. Now, of course, it was all so

27

endearing — retrospective forgiveness laid bare all sins as fond remembrances.

He moved to the kitchen table suddenly and sat there as all those machines worked. Public radio spoke to the world of America — serial killers, pre-war, post-war, new political scandals.

"Idiots, such idiots," and then smiled at his own words, as if acknowledging the idiot he was in being like them.

Somewhere I could hear inside him that he knew I was still around. He spoke of it with Jennifer too, and she was aware of me also. This human instinct for the spiritual world, "beyond," fascinated me, and I wondered in my unfamiliar limbo if this perhaps was the very reason for my presence. I was here because we all wanted me to be here. There were television programs about the other side, books galore, psychics, visionaries, and all, and all. The living world is filled with the dead world, everybody wants to know about it, and here I was, willing to give of what I could.

The giving was an opportunity for me, and a learning for him, and therefore for the whole world. Ah, how profoundly justified I felt in this quest that I didn't even know the meaning of.

Gideon stood again and moved without purpose through the kitchen; turned off the lights and then turned them on again, stroked the flowers that stood on the ledge around the stove, stroked Tashy with his foot as the animal nuzzled his shins.

He seemed always to come back to me like a homing pigeon, routing through the sky here and there but always landing on my shoulder with his thoughts and emotions. He seemed unable to leave, but I wasn't one to talk. I was certainly not leaving, in fact all this was beginning to become a pleasure, though my heart swelled, my feelings, such as they were, obsessed about his condition. What had I done to him in destroying the last vestiges of my existence in the body? How selfish I had managed to be when our lives together were already so heavily damaged. I could have shared my death with him but chose to engineer it through chemical additives. How stupid can you be? But I also saw that it was not stupid, but merely inevitable, and in any event now I had the opportunity to make amends.

He continued to wander through the house, down into the main living room — a huge vaulted, church-like redwood-roofed dominion that contained our lives with all the antique and stylish furniture we had originally brought from London.

Yes, in that moment I remembered London too, where Jennifer had been so often by our sides. We had lived there for six years together in a moody apartment in Hampstead, where the passing traffic had grimed the lace curtains, and the Irish bombers blew up the local fire station.

We had warmed our hearts together in front of open fires, got drunk together with over-charged wine, while Harvey Nichols and Harrods offered recuperation from dronedom, and taxi-fatigue, and World's End brought the past to an unaffordable present.

These memories flooded my being, wherever it was, and helped me to formulate time and place, especially for Gideon, for he shared what I owned, and our togetherness right now was everything for me.

"Thanks. I'm going to work a bit, I'm going to try to run away somewhere out of sight." I got up from my desk at Berkeley.

"Do you feel she's watching?" Jennifer also stood, behind her desk. Was this a gesture to show me more of her body? She knew how her body turned men's heads, but I turned my face away and opened the door.

"Yes, for sure she watches. If any of this is real, she never takes her eyes off me." I said this with a small smile, as though I knew what Jennifer's movements meant. She blushed and sat down quickly. I closed the door so silently and so delicately there was hardly a click.

Jennifer did not tell me the other story just then; a story that she remembered as though it were one of those moments created by a lifelong condition or a moment learned at the bosom of her mother, so vivid was it. This was a tale to tell, but she didn't tell it, and swore she never would, for if she did, it would leave her.

It had been a hot-hot day. She remembered it as one of those California summer mornings when the "fog" fails to come in over the hills from the ocean. Temperatures were over 100 degrees — and after three days of sweltering everyone was cursing not having installed air conditioning again this year.

Jennifer walked from her car to the Depot in Mill Valley. She passed the ball-playing youths and stumbled over the plump-breasted, spoiled girls escaping from Tam High, chattering with that innocence unwieldy in such bodies, well into womanhood. She watched the California young in their isolated, embodied freedom, and wondered why she had stayed in Berkeley, where the minds prevailed and the clothes betrayed. She headed for a croissant and coffee, planning to sit quietly, unknown to the locals, for a moment of oblivious absence. But as she approached the small swinging gateway of the Depot café, everything stopped and she stood transfixed, literally paralyzed by what she saw.

She had known us forever. She had known Nicki before the Big Bang! She had known the tragedy of Nicki's death, and the dreadful bereavement that had followed, and she had known our story thereafter. It was only days since the death, and no one had started to recover — Nicki had been such a darling, such a lover and friend, such a beauty to observe in the normal range of human life — far better, more dramatic, more talented than most of us. All negatives were forgotten in the light of Nicki's memory. She may have been hot-tempered, wildly Spanish. She may have been obsessively ambitious, relentlessly driving. She may have been moody and emotionally unbalanced — whoever cared now about these things? Only the sun shone over her memory.

And there we stood together between two ancient trees just before the outdoor tables. Just after Nicki's death, just as I began my bereavement and loss — we stood alone together in the doorway of the Mill Valley book store — alone together, our faces skin-to-skin, our hands gently caressing, our love soft and real. But she was dead.

Jennifer had remained there watching this scene, she later told me. She was happy to see that Nicki was obviously not dead. She was delighted to see Nicki's hand rested on my shoulder, her head gently inclined to my cheek, talking to me in that way that only the most intimate lovers can, and between these trees that somehow she had not noticed before.

Jennifer felt curiously possessive. This was the woman she had loved as her best friend before we fell in love. She wanted to share in this return to life — be part of what was going on. Maybe Nicki would explain to her what was happening. She'd recovered, been mistakenly diagnosed, in a coma or something. Perhaps she would explain to Jennifer how she stood so close to me, how she managed such intimacy if she was dead.

But then, after Jennifer turned her head to observe the others present in this gathering of living souls — somehow to compare them — Nicki was gone, and only I stood there alone, and the trees were not quite the same trees — not as old or unusual as the ones she had seen us between before. She could not approach me and ask the obvious question, "were you with Nicki just now?" How foolish she would feel, and yet this was all she wanted to say in the world. She wanted to approach the groups around the tables and ask them, "Did you see her? Was she here?" "Did she hold his hand so fondly? Was he taken in by her kisses and caresses?"

They would deny. "No, I saw only a man." "No, there was no sweet woman there just now." And they would stare offhandedly at Jennifer, a look of uncertainty in their eyes. Maybe she was not quite all there for asking, and besides, from the way she dressed, she couldn't be from these parts.

Wasn't that the strangest thing? But she had to accept. It had only been the quickest, most passing image — a man and woman touching, a couple in the slightest embrace near those trees just for the tenderest and slightest moment. Who would know if it was true?

And yet she had seen it. Jennifer had witnessed this scene and could not yet tell it, even forever, for she knew and yet she could not know.

As she stood there in the Mill Valley heat, suddenly it became heavy and oppressive. The people seemed uncertain, almost as though they moved with her experience. There were shadows where there shouldn't be, complexity where simplicity should have prevailed. Such slight impressions changed the world for her.

Jennifer stepped back, forgot the croissant and coffee, and returned to her car.

But what did Nicki remember? What was in all this for her? Death transforms, it does not kill. All that she knew before the veil, she knew now. All that she felt, cared for, feared, doubted, remained so now. The only change was that she existed a step outside me. The animals saw her, the trees danced for her, the air caressed her, the smells bore fruit for her; everything the same, better even, for Nicki sensed more sensitively, touched more sublimely, heard everything, even thoughts and feelings. She could see a whole history, a whole past. She could assume an entire future without it imposing. She could touch tension without personal pain, and anxiety without obsession. Her dictums were free while her personality took note without imprisonment. Her identity was gone, for she had no body to guard it. All her old attachments and desires still carried weight in her heart for Gideon. How privileged was I in this? How pained was she?

Meanwhile she watched the being that carried all the negative, all the dreams, and all the purpose. I ate my toast, drank my tea, gazing out at the keen grass and tall foliage of the land about the house. My face was musing, my thoughts moving slowly over the necessities of the day. Nicki thanked whatever existence offered for the fact that I was not ground down by her death. She wished also that I would hurt too, for her absence. I did both, it seemed, obliging her and her close call. I wandered through the rooms of the house sometimes — this time — and simply stroked the surfaces, felt the feelings that brought her back to me, and although these moments were often intensely painful and deeply personal, they also somehow washed me of doubt and pain, like a true absolution; a priest's confession, so that I could manage to return to some vestige of normality. Normality? What the hell was that?

But still somewhere there was that shadow she could not fathom, something darker than she, something that hovered beside her in the realms of the dead that she had not yet explored — places that lay waiting for her, places of such uncertain colors that to contemplate them was already too much. There was something there — something she did not want to discover.

That night the heavy spring rain fell on the redwood roof above our bedroom. I woke and thrashed about for the clock beside the bed; the clock that still had a picture of Nicki beside it. The picture had been taken in a hotel somewhere we had been on a vacation during the early days of our arrival in California. We had spent several scattered weeks together discovering places like Mount Shasta where the Native Americans had left their spirits on the mountainside and around the lakes. I remember the silences and the spooky feelings these places evoked in us, and how we scuttled back down to the Bay in the old Jaguar that leaked from all its orifices. We'd been happy — lots of laughter and snuggling, and everything seemed to affect us so profoundly.

As I lay there among the crumpled sheets that night, squinting at the photograph in the half-light of the full moon, the roof cracked loudly and lightning suddenly flashed, bringing an eeriness into the house. I repositioned Nicki's battered pillow so I could sit more upright in the bed, and in that instant I caught the smell of her — oh God, so profound, so much evoked in a smell — a kind of perfume of my deepest feelings. Raising my head to try to catch more of it, there came another lightning flash. I swear that she appeared then, behind the image in the frame, backed up by the silvered light of the moon and the sharpness of the lightning. She stood there for an instant, or so my heart and soul convinced my mind, behind the picture. Thunder crashed in upon me during that moment and my heart flew out of my body in a rising crescendo of doubt and hurt, fear and excitement, like both sides of a worn coin that flipped above my head.

And then the calm. Was she there or was she not? My head fell back on the pillow again, and the fragrance of her presence was as real as if she lay beside me. So much of togetherness with another is shaped by physical intimacy, and yet, within a deep-seated love affair that has lasted many years, there is often as much intimacy in aloneness. Somehow in that awesome moment, within the calm of the passing storm that flaked across the sky above the cracking roof, I was left with the silence of the rain; that warm, soft falling rain, securing our hearts together in distance from one another. Perhaps her form, in some form, lay beside me, for I knew so much of her beauty and her presence then. The chasm that separated us also brought us closer.

The Mill-Valley phone rang. Gideon answered quickly.

"Hi, George. Yes, I'm okay. Don't ask." Tetchy as always with anyone who investigated him. "I'll be at the office in an hour or so." He behaved the reserved English public-school-educated only child. Second approaches brought greater compassion, but essentially he was the superior, the aristocrat — smiling and polite but distant and unapproachable. This characteristic had always fascinated me. How did he do it? I was Spanish by contrast, blustering and aggressive, open and passionate — willing to engage at any level as long as it suited me. He, on the other hand, drank gallons of tea, walked privately as if in contemplation of greater things than any of us simple mortals could engage. His frame enhanced this capability. He was tall and broadly built, a little overweight — barn-house-doorish. His presence dominated and sold itself without effort. Others tended to respect and trust him, so that he rarely needed to engage beyond the necessity of the moment. This is not to say he was insensitive, in fact his internal management was dangerously close to disturbed, needing constant protection from the outside confrontations of life, and yet he seemed always able enough in matters of survival and work. The eyes told it all. Those eyes that darted away from damage, but closed in on pain. Those eyes that dwelled on children and brought tears, eyes that noticed everything, remembered too much.

He hovered a few more minutes around his breakfast dishes and then reluctantly returned to the bedroom. His cleaners would repair the damage that previously I had insisted upon fixing.

He stripped naked to wash, testing the water in that huge shower stall we had so often shared. His tall body had grown slimmer. The belly had reduced to almost nothing now, and there weren't those once-muscular breasts any more, nor the rounded sides to his stomach — handles, as some call them, not I. His hair was still not gray, but thick and blond, though he was more than fifty now. The beard showed white at some points, but signs of aging somehow didn't touch him as they did other men. I wandered if he was being as kind to himself as I had been, as I had nagged during our lives together. I prided myself on helping to preserve him, always imagining that he would die before I did. I was twenty years younger than he, after all, how could I have imagined anything other than guiding his last breath in my arms, yet he had guided mine in his.

I watched those powerful, tree-trunk legs as he showered, watched him slowly vanish behind the steam. Where would all this go? What could I do for him? How could I make him know of me truly again? And this enlisted a certain attitude. I regarded the living as inferior — needing help from me. Why did this strike me so? Was it really true that the living somehow suffered a "Christian" fate of pain, duty, and guilt? Did the dead — reborn so close — have something special to give to the living? It was certainly inbred within my living soul to suppose this to be true. I saw the agony of abandonment on his face, the anxiety of expectation, the doubt of preservation. All this framed within flesh. Conversely I felt my own freedom — I had no body to contain any of these emotions; hormonal changes, physical entrapments. I existed still, it seemed, with a vestige of past lives that essentially had no bearing on my future, whatever that would be. All I needed to do was rid myself of human memory, and I would float somewhere in this new world, probably discovering more of it by discarding the past.

Instead, I chose to maintain a vigil around this single living human, identifying with his agony, his hanging there within the pale of doubt and pleasure. Why should I choose such conditions in the midst of "higher" things? Answers were subject to that same condition — I loved him! What higher thing is there?

The streets toward his office were crowded — unusually for Marin. Some event-filled spaces that would normally have been occupied only by a few hippies and middle-class mothers — organic conservatives, unwilling to be rushed on their inevitable ways. A market lined the street at the bottom of the hill on Miller Avenue — the main drag into Mill Valley. I guarded his driving, watched for danger, watched also his blond thick hair blow as he drove the little coup I'd recently acquired and loved. He only took this car now, snug in the seat I had half filled, pressed back to its maximum length from the pedals. He moved his body from side to side as though cuddled in my lap, smelling my scent on the leather, stroking the residues of my skin on the wheel. He breathed deeply, I heard, sniffing for evidence of my passing. He cried as he drove, but the gushing wind dried the tears from his face.

The traffic came to a standstill. He was in a hurry, though this was not unusual. One of his most peculiar failings was that he needed always to be getting

somewhere else. Arrival never happened, for his urge
for departure overtook the journey before it ended,
and he was exhorting me to leave and on to the
next destination. Astrologers told me it was an Aries
quality, this constant race for the next starting line.

Frustration made him sweat lightly, made him grind
his teeth and curse behind them, silently. So I cleared
the road for him. Suddenly the traffic all seemed to
go in different directions, stopping at gas stations,
turning off to park behind the market, speeding up
with the spaces I concurred, waving him on as though
he were an ambulance, his inner siren clanging. The
street he entered was also suddenly empty. He pushed
his foot to the floor, that glorious Mercedes engine
gashing grooves in the tarmac, freeing his spirit
for forgetfulness. He took the freeway, freely away,
seventy, eighty, ninety, no cops to bother him, for I
sent them to solve greater crimes than those of a man
struggling to face up to the death of his lifetime lover.
I pitched the sun down his shirt to warm his chest,
the wind through his hair and over his drowning face,
held the rubber to the road and the engine to its gears,
raised the volume of the roaring pistons, and made
a boy of him again, just there, just then — a boy of
him again.

# TWO

Gideon stood uneasily, his right hand resting on the sill of his office window, sensing the unpredictable vibrations of the faults that kept all Bay Area residents on their toes and visitors in perplexity. When we'd first moved to the Bay Area five years before, his parents had professed concern for the killer-quakes. Our choice to live in Marin County reduced the risks, but working in Berkeley doubled them during working hours.

He considered. Why was Jennifer behaving in that way? Did she think she needed to comfort him with more than her old friendship? The sensations her attentions had produced in him troubled his heart.

His thoughts tumbled between what to do about the situation and an intense sense of regret that he could not tell me about it. I longed for him to understand that he *was* telling me, but my powerlessness to let him know made me hot — I knew heat — a sensation imagined rather than experienced, yet real in itself. He let go of the sill and walked to one of the electronic sensing machines that lined one side of his office. The vibrations of the fault line seemed to have echoed into his body, for as he touched the sensors on the machine it felt as though he was transferring the power from the ground. He flipped a switch, put the headphones on, and attached one of the sensor pads to his chest, another to his forehead, and a third to the pulse on his wrist, taping this one into a secure position. He sat in the padded chair and pressed his back against the sensor pads embedded into the rest, taking up a familiar position.

"Are you there, Nicki? Please speak to me, Nicki, I miss you so much." Tears welled up into his eyes and fell quickly down his cheeks and into his beard. He wiped them free to prevent any interference with the sensitive equipment, but his eyes insisted, the tear ducts unable to respond to his determined attempts at negating his feelings. He had tried this so many times in recent weeks — tried to find solace in the professional, tried to create a belief mechanism that would set down an earthing of his grieving soul. He questioned whether he could be serious about his attempts to make contact with a spirit so close to his heart — did it require some objectivity? Would he need to come through the pain to a place that would permit a more scientific analysis of his situation before he could be successful? Was he somehow like a doctor who attended a close relative — unable to perform his techniques in the face of too much feeling? Or was all this an excuse for the truth — that there was no spirit to contact, and all he did was imagine through hope the fantasy of existence beyond the veil?

The tears took over and he pulled off the headphones, ripping the wrist pad from his arm and directing the hopeless hand to his face to cup the falling stream of sadness. As he did so, and at first without seeing it, the monitor on the sensor casing blipped suddenly, visualizing energy. It blipped again, this time loudly, and his eyes quickly cleared as his heart skipped a beat. Behind him, the window opened and swung back, a gust of wind bursting through the room and blowing his hair wildly across his forehead. At the same moment I traced my fingers over his face and pushed the hair back, gently leaning over him and kissing his forehead — a kiss like no other, my presence in the wind drying the tears instantly. His head fell back against the chair back and his mouth fell open in astonishment. His whole body experienced a shiver of energy that quivered like the bow of a hunter and engulfed him in delight.

"Oh God, Nicki, oh God, where are you? Please tell me, where are you?" Hardly daring to move or believe, he remained where he was, the muscle of his neck tensing now, his eyes wide open and his heart competing with the vibrating ground.

"It's a quake." The floor began to move. Papers and books tilted from the shelves and desks, crashing to the ground. For a split second it was as though the whole building was going to fall about him and a sense of alarm so deep within him rose to the surface bringing panic like nothing he had experienced before.

Suddenly, without the slightest hesitation he stood up and raised his arms into the air. At the top of his voice, as loud as it could carry he shouted a single word, "STOP." And it did, for I made it, right there and then.

The books and items on the shelves hit the ground, and the sounds of the cracking earth made their point. Chaos flew through the air like a flock of rowdy birds, this then followed by an extraordinary and sudden stillness. There was literally a pause in life as though a gap opened up between two moments, and the gap was greater than it should have been. It was almost as though time stopped, and he was left suspended in a widening moment without volition. And then this too stopped.

He turned from his stance of prophet and master of the universe and, clutching both arms around his own shoulders, moved quickly toward the door, aiming for the doorframe where some safety might prevail in that split second, imagining in his uncertainty that the quake would resurge and bring him down. But before reaching the handle he hesitated. Had he really done this? Had he been responsible for something that he could never achieve? Ridiculous. What human could prevail over the massive power of Mother Earth Herself?

Sensing something else, Gideon turned again back toward the inside of the room and saw me standing there before him simple, small, Nicki-shaped, slightly translucent.

He gasped, frozen, everything entirely still about him. The quake was quiet, not even the slightest hint of vibration — dots only his breath came fast and his heart beat faster, his face entirely white until a smile spread over it like the sun had risen.

"Oh Nick — it *is* you isn't it — Nick, please God make it be you...."

I remained there for a few moments, allowing my body to shine, the skin brazen, the color outlined in light, the smells and tastes briefly available to him. There was a peace between us that had only ever existed in the last year of our lives together, before I became seriously ill — a friendship unrepeatable in those moments when life is replete and desireless. Here, I copied these designs, these God-given works of art, just for him, just for now. There was no asking in his chest, no question in his throat, only deep thankfulness and poetry that outlined him in a pale, organic blue aura of love's labors declined.

We didn't speak but smiled. We didn't move but embraced. I gave all there was to give and he drank it down until I could sustain it no longer. Gideon quickly became aware of sounds outside his office. Chaos had broken into a full dash for the exit. The faculty building backed onto a large grass square where everyone now stood in huddled groups, discussing their fears and repairing their dignities. Jennifer was in a small circle of friends, her head craning to discover Gideon's whereabouts.

"Anyone seen Gideon — Gideon Falwall, anyone? Gideon, where are you?" She finally yelled at the top of her voice. Silence came and heads began to turn in all directions.

"I heard him shouting upstairs in the lab," someone yelled back.

" 'Stop,' he said . . . I heard it loud and clear — and you know what? It did." Everyone began to laugh, the panic of the experience suddenly cleansing into reaction. At that precise moment he appeared at the exit to the building, standing on the top step, his whole body shaking uncontrollably. Almost the entire crowd, about forty people, quickly surged to the bottom of the steps, Jennifer in the lead. She and four others dashed up the steps and grabbed him as he stumbled and fell. They took his body, now limp, and carried him down to the grass.

"Get a doctor for Christ's sake. Maybe he's hurt. . . . " Jennifer rubbed his wrist, not knowing what this could possibly do, but assuring herself in the act. His eyes opened and stared at her.

"I saw her, Jennifer, I saw her . . . she kissed me, I can still feel it."

"Oh God, Gideon, are you okay?" She continued to rub his hand.

"She kissed me . . . she kissed me. . . . "

The college medic checked Gideon's condition and attended to a few other cuts and bruises among the staff and students. No major problems had resulted from the quake — which had lasted for precisely ten seconds. Talk of Gideon's loud command took up some part of the remaining afternoon and then was forgotten. In something of a daze I watched him driven back to our home by a delighted but very cautious student, the sports Mercedes trailing behind Jennifer's car. He had never allowed anyone to even stroke the vehicle before this day.

Jennifer had begged him to come back to her house where she offered to watch over him for a while, but he was far too excited and exhausted to want attention even from her — indeed, it seemed in his mind, especially from her. I liked this. It was typical of him and suitable under the circumstances. I had worked miracles, after all, to attract his attention.

Once free of others, he found one of his favorite places on the upper deck at the front of the house, inside the hot tub. The sky reflected its own miracle, and deer foraged the acreage around the house, wrecking flowers, weeds, and roots. Early spring burgeoned with the mixed West Coast climate, alternating between bright sun and delirious rain and what Californian's referred to as "fog." This late morning was ideal for the tub, and he did well with his thoughts and feelings while surrounded by bubbling hot water. There was an aura of excitement around him that almost made the bubbles burst bigger and faster. He had seen me, been kissed by his lifelong lover, felt my energy pass through him, felt me stop an earthquake, for heaven's sake! What was this dream engulfing his life when he was supposed simply to be in mourning? He cried into the water when he thought of the grief that all this brought to his heart. But he laughed when he imagined that what had happened in the lab might have been true. Could it be true, or was he just crazy and deluded? So many tears, so much emotion, laughter and sadness, all sending tears to the earth. Was there truly any difference between them? And if I had appeared before him that day, and it wasn't some delusion, then what is the difference between life and death? Could it possibly be that they might somehow reunite and my death become meaningless, or still better — meaningful?

I dressed quickly after a rapid shower. I hadn't eaten since the previous morning, before the earthquake. It was as though the events of that day had given me a shot of energy that made the normal demands of life completely irrelevant. I'd slept in the chair beside the hot tub the afternoon before, and woken to the dimming light of dusk and the rustle of breezes. I'd attempted sleep after that, but I tossed and turned much of the night, getting up to find entertainment in music or my computer — anything to make the night pass, but it flatly refused, taking twice as long as any previous night. I couldn't call anyone anywhere. People in Europe — my mother and father, my few remaining friends, my first wife, Jane, my kids, all slept soundly eight hours ahead of me, until around two in the morning when I knew my son Charles would be at his office in London. I couldn't call him at home early in the morning because I knew the flurry Charles got into in his rush for the office each day. My daughter, Amanda, would be at her boyfriend's flat, and I felt awkward at calling into her love nest.

Everything had changed in that instant in my office. Though many questions arose about the reality of the experience, a certain new program had begun to run in my life that brought tremendous excitement, both personally and professionally. I had studied the enigmas of the paranormal for decades without much palpable evidence, and I had grown accustomed to the groans of doubt from associates, college faculty professors, and grant distributors alike. The study of "ghosts," as most outsiders termed our work, was roughly akin to that undertaken by exobiologists and UFO freaks. Nobody really believed in what we expected to discover, though most longed to hear of solid proof that something existed either out there in space or out there in heaven and hell.

The nearest anyone got to results was the discovery of ultra sensitivity to psychic phenomena. Certain "gifted" individuals managed to confirm our hopes, but that only occurred once in a blue moon when the occasional student displayed irregular abilities to name hidden playing cards or experienced events that seemed just as likely to be parlor games. Then there were the performing psychics, who invariably turned out to be nothing more than sensitive to human thought and memory — helped along by some good background research into the lives of subjects desperate to meet with "the other side."

The Faculty for the Study of Para-Phenomenology (FSPP, also commonly called "Fssssp, don't tell anyone what we found") had struggled like hell to get grants to build equipment, only to discover that if they were honorably precise in their diagnostics, blips resulted largely from natural activity in the earth or the electroencephala of the subjects. No one with the smallest amount of scientific background had really seen or spoken to a spirit or any other form of post organic existence — until yesterday, that is. Today, I was not only convinced of what I saw but enormously frightened that I had done no more than experience a hallucination brought on by an entirely natural phenomenon — the quake. How easy it was to rationalize. How impossible to prove the unprovable.

In my experience it seemed that science and the paranormal were fundamentally at extreme odds, and if the world of spirits existed it eschewed the world of human science as if by default. Laboratory proof was a human endeavor that contained, in its very atomic formation, an inability to witness a world that I, and many of my colleagues, believed to be lacking in all facets of the rules set up to achieve such proof.

The doubting Thomases never, of course, stopped to consider that human experiences might be the key to the presence of the spirit, just as it was the key in the processes of quantum theory — that the veil separating the two was so thin as to be potentially invisible.

In this way I rationalized my emotional pain, and my grief. In this way I found channels to be in touch with the one thing in my life that had sustained me for so long — Nicki and her life. Her life and her death, perhaps, were linked to me as strongly as ever they were when she groaned as I woke her too early, and brushed my hair in the morning, bathing my postures with good sense and planting my seeds of doubt in good ground to flower with certainty.

It somehow astonished me, if astonishment was mine to feel, how the lightest kiss had been planted on his forehead at all, and how the earthquake had stopped, as it seemed to. I had not set out to do any of what had been done, though I knew that I was the vehicle for it. I had not engineered my appearance in our bedroom during the flashing storm from the "other side," though I knew that I had been there, nevertheless.

I had not set out at all in any direction, for I did not walk or fly or run through my life after death. I simply appeared or disappeared somewhere beyond the veil, and situations occurred without apparent intention by me alone. And yet there was a kind of willingness in me for these events to occur, which I suppose in a way was an intention. In these early days it was still very confusing, for I knew that I wanted to give Gideon powers and joys rather than suffering, and yet I made no specific plans or efforts to facilitate events. In some way, I guess, I was simply a part of the intention, a nightingale at night in a plan that was far bigger than I. And yet that still wasn't right, for I also had the sense that there wasn't anything bigger, just something else — something I could not yet encompass as my own. I remember, when I lived in my body, there were events that felt like they weren't "mine," but which occurred outside me, beyond me — like writing stories that when I read them again seemed somehow to have emerged from outside me. This is the closest I can get to describing my world. I could love and fear, doubt and delight, as I had done in my body. There were other spirits around me that I guessed I could make contact with, but it was somehow all done for me, and with me. And the doing was instant — as came the wish, so came the act.

Everything Gideon undertook, on the other hand, appeared deliberate, or at least apparently deliberate to *him,* yet as I watched him progress through his separation from me and the grief that occupied his heart, it became more and more apparent that in fact his actions — though formulated by what seemed a solid body and solid things around him were also not truly functioning because of a will or deliberation. He was energy, just as I was energy. Life in life coincided just as it did in death. The thunderstorm and the bright lightning happened during the same instant that he woke to the sound of rain, smelled my fragrance on the pillow, and gazed bleakly at the photograph. The acceptance and awareness of the kiss coincided with the beginning and end of the quake, and the equipment that monitored his brush with the spirit world and his brush with earth herself.

Nothing happens in isolation. Everything coincides with everything else. And so his grief for my passing came alongside his yearning for my return. His patronage of the beating of the earth's violent heart grew precisely as the beating of his own heart dealt with its shame and doubt, its pain and fear.

And so too in all this comes the final wisdom and understanding that life and death — both these profound energy forms — also coincide and are one and the same.

At 2:00 a.m. I called my son Charles — ten o'clock London time, but he was already in meetings, so I returned to bed and tried to sleep again without

success, for the well of energy in my body and mind could not slow down.

The morning eventually arrived — laboriously, painfully. After dressing, I grabbed a briefcase with nothing in it, vaguely wondering what I would need it for. I left the car keys on the front hall table and forgot to press the garage door opener that lay on the same shelf, even when I had returned for them. I thought of how fit I would get bounding up and down the stairs, forgetting every item I needed, and taking the ones I did not. I had seen Nicki. I had seen her, seen her, been kissed by her, and I would see her again if it were the last thing I ever did.

I would drive to Berkeley. I considered this plan. I would go to the lab and try an experiment. It seemed that Nicki's appearance had been related to a dramatic event — the quake. If I could somehow electronically duplicate that event, and I knew I could, then perhaps I would be able to recreate the conditions that would make it possible to see her, or at least make contact with her, once more. The quake would have registered and been recorded on the ECG in the office, and the drama of the event was already bursting from my own body. I would use a combination of the two forms of energy to bring about another connection. I had carefully thought through the emotional responses that I had felt during the process, writing down detailed descriptions of everything that had happened to me during those few seconds. This was a normal part of my work, and I had spent years perfecting the processes of how the body and chemistry of the mind and feelings performed under every possible set of events. This was my pioneering effort, and I had spoken of it during several of my lectures. That my success was intrinsic to the art of observation as much as any science, only the observation was almost exclusively that of the inner life of the individual involved in the event. Phenomenology was never objective, only subjective, and the scientist *was* the event in totality.

I had seen her. There was little doubt of that. But had I seen her because she had caused the event, or because I had, or because the earthquake had triggered false conditions brought about in conjunction with my eager mind, or what? And more important still — would it happen again?

But I never left the house. Somehow I couldn't turn this experience into a real practice — a real experiment. So I climbed back out of the small car and walked back up the outside stairs to the house again, undressed and climbed back into the hot tub.

I flapped my hands about in the water like a small boy searching for his floating toys. A big crow flew across the sky and landed on the deck fencing, ruffled its wings and tail, adjusting ready to depart again, then turned toward me and tilted its head, letting out a special squawk as though questioning my line of reasoning. "Don't be stupid," it seemed to say. "Of course she did it, and so did you — one for the other, together," it continued. "Get on with your new life with a living spirit." The huge bird then hopped onto the side of the tub and motioned its beak, evidently quite unafraid, its head moving from side to side in an obvious gesture of frustration at human ignorance. Nothing could be more obvious — only you dumb humans would question something so simple and clear. In a gesture of bored irritation, the bird turned tail in one hop, deposited a dollop of lime from its rear into the water, and flew gracefully away from the scene.

I began to think that I was going insane.

As I watch all this confusion in him between science and reality, I felt strangely happy. I had somehow facilitated quite a lot for the time being — a miracle and a "talking bird." Pretty good for such a fresh spirit. No one had come around, perched on *my* shoulder, and told *me* off for what I was doing. Fate, or whatever it was, seemed on my side. I wondered how long this would endure. Perhaps when it all became easy I would no longer wish to do it. But the thought made me consider my place in all this. In fact, I had noticed that the moment I attached myself to the connection I had with Gideon's life, the connection I had with my own would instantly come into question. It was as if my world reflected his world — though also, in this parity I assumed we were separate, and it was becoming clear that we were not. There was no contact exactly, but the separation was nothing much more than a construct that each of us created.

I looked around me, but all I saw when I was so concentrated on him was his surroundings. I tried to smell my own existence, independent (as the scientist would say) of his, but all I smelled was his body, the hot water, the birdlime, the flowers in the garden, the fear and doubt of human existence. How could I prove that he existed independent of me? What would the grant-check-signers say to my request for funds? The same, no doubt, as they said to him.

He slept in the chair beside the grimy pool of water. I cleaned it, sweeping away my bird-friend's lime. The bird-friend squawked from across the forest, still watching me hovering over my man, laughing in his bird-beard.

# THREE

Jennifer fussed around my office door as I burst in and started setting up the machines opposite my desk. I'd finally made my way to the faculty office.

"Are you all right, Gideon? What did you mean yesterday when you said you had seen her? You said it over and over. Who did you see? Gideon? Are you listening to me?"

One of Jennifer's most irritating habits was to insist on being heard, and I had noticed recently that this urgent pestering merely made me want to ignore her all the more.

"Nicki. I saw Nicki. Who did you think I meant?" I dragged the ECG and its small monitor further toward the front of the table and tussled with the various cables that attached to it. The earthquake had left a muddle in its wake, but everything seemed more or less intact.

"Did you stop that quake, Gideon? I heard you shout. Or did Nicki?"

I paused and finally turned toward Jennifer. "You don't miss much, do you?" I was genuinely impressed by her jump into the unknown.

"You forget. I've known you two a long time. I wouldn't put it passed you both to come up with a way to get back together again, even beyond the grave." This made me laugh. Her face was so serious when she said it!

"Yes, but that's a big jump to making miracles. Isn't it?"

"Not really. One miracle leads, after all, to another. The Vatican only awards sainthood to those who make two." She smiled impishly.

"Go away, Jennifer, I have urgent things to do. I'll call you later." Jennifer bobbed her head the way they do in India, and closed my door behind her.

I attached myself to the ECG monitor and turned on the screen. I reran the tapes from the previous day until the jagged, darting lines on the screen registered the huge rise in energy produced by the quake. It was all there — at least the mechanical, external electronics were available. Now all I had to do was elucidate my own emotional responses. At first this seemed tricky, as the recording had taken note of the greater force of the quake, overwhelming the recording of my heart, breathing, and internal responses of the previous day. How would I know which was which? Set against the sudden and dramatic pulses of the quake, my own body responses seemed miniscule. It was a bit like trying to separate an ECG heart reading from the dropping of a bomb.

Narrowing down the pulses from the recording, I attempted to figure out which was which, but the pulses were so intimately entangled that it seemed impossible to find my personal recordings. Eventually, after an hour of fiddling unsuccessfully, I tried the audio monitor, hoping that I might delineate the heart beat itself as an independent presence against the sounds of the quake and the noises of my breathing and voice.

I had cried out several times during the event, and these sounds added to the general chaos that hid the more important emotional responses of my body — effects that I hoped to use to recreate the story. It took time, but there were numerous audio responses recorded that might have been relevant to what I supposed to be my physical presence in the drama of the previous day.

Somewhere in there I heard the crashing of the window and the gust of wind that had blown through the room. There was a particular swishing sound. It was very faint and it bore little resemblance to anything I had remembered in my written analysis whilst in the recall session I had undertaken during my restless night. There was also another sound — very far away and deeply embedded in the din of the quake, which I could hardly detect, but it resembled what seemed to be, could it possibly be, a kiss? The digitized sound occurred very close to my face around the area of my forehead. It was so faint that I feared it

might simply lead me astray in my scientific study —
might turn out to be no more than the digital recording
of the falling of dust on my head, or a shifting swirl
of wind that passed through my hair. And there was
this too — almost as though the gust of wind had
pushed my hair forward, and then something else had
reversed the trend and swept it back again from my
forehead, all in a split second.

Growing fascinated and slightly obsessed by these
faint and unlikely sounds, my years of training told
me to concentrate on the minutia of the process
that had unfolded. The personal, the intimate, the
inner responses almost always indicated more than
the major external, less personal events as to what
had actually been occurring. I played back the tape
again, narrowing the beams of sound still further
with the complex and sensitive equipment. The loud
pulses of the quake, the crashing shelves of books
and papers and the opening window, were regressed
into the background, and gradually I managed to pull
up the most delicate pulses so that they were hugely
magnified.

I watched him at work — his intense concentration
bringing beads of sweat to his forehead and neck.
Loving this man's passion, I blew gently on him to
cool his body, coating his skin in the gentlest breeze
as he worked. As I did so, he suddenly lifted his eyes

above the spectacles he wore for close reading, and then lifted his head. But he shook it and returned to the screen and headphones, so as not to disrupt his concentration. The sounds were now clearer. There was definitely a counter-movement across his head that followed the heavy gust of wind that blew in through the burst-open window, and this was followed by a very brief touch against his forehead with that quality which exists only in the kiss.

I blew across his forehead again as it formed more moisture, slightly harder this time, and watched the sweat evaporate, drifting, as it did, seen from my bizarre world, into trails of gentle, floating humidity above his head. This time, he lifted his hand and touched his brow, turning toward where I stood beside him. "Nick? Is that you?" He remained frozen as I blew on his hand. "Nick, you're there aren't you? I know you're there Nick? Don't tease me. Don't do what you always used to do, please Nicki?" His hand floated hesitantly down again to the knobs and buttons of the audio monitor, his heart thundering, his mind trying to bring him back to good sense.

I leaned forward and raised the volume of the recording that had just been made of my cooling breath. The machine both replayed and recorded simultaneously, so now he had two separate sounds emitting from it — one from the previous day and one from the previous minute. He gasped, and leaned over to listen again, but I prevented it, touching his hand with mine so gently that it felt to him like a tiny insect landing on his skin.

"What should I do, Nick? Are you trying to help me? What should I do?"

I took his hand in mine. There was no doubt now in his mind and senses that he was being guided. I took also his other hand and gently swiveled his body round in the chair so that he sat with his back to the machinery. He allowed it, his face pale and his body shaking slightly, everything in that tender, uncanny moment bringing his deepest concentration into the present.

There was no plan in my movements, no method in my madness. I simply followed some instinct that existed in my part of his world, to demonstrate that he was not fooling himself, and that his hopes of connection with me were entirely justified. I did not know why I needed to do this, or what would result from it, but as I leaned further forward, and kissed his mouth, it was the kiss of eternity, a kiss that would change his life and his view of life, a kiss to end all kisses, for it aroused him sexually, warmed his deepest emotions, and delved into his heart to places that no living human could have discovered. It was the kiss of an angel, an angel in love.

When I stood back before him, he saw me again, his eyes filling with the tears of astonishment and response. I was beyond love and doubt, beyond any normal human reaction, and in that moment we both existed in the same realm, once again joined as we had been in our lives together. I knew that it was the beginning of something intensely important to us — I the living ghost, and he the living spirit, two as one in heaven.

As though mesmerized, he turned eventually, still in a kind of daze, and switched off all the machinery. It was simple now. He knew that for the moment at least, I was available to him, but that volition for our contact had to arise from me, though of course his continued desire for it played an essential part in the equation. He knew it as well as I did, and it became clear to me that this had been the purpose of my moves toward him that day.

The miracle that existed in all life began for him there with that kiss, and over the next few days grew in intensity, and power — the start of a miracle that I perpetrated, and he performed.

Unable to do anything approaching work, I returned to the house, abandoning poor Jennifer to her confusion. I crept out of the office and dashed to the little Mercedes, pumping the gas pedal to the floor once on the freeway. My sense of excitement was almost too much to bear, and I sang songs I had forgotten I loved, which somehow were chosen one after the other on every radio station. For the first time in months I saw the glorious ocean passing by, pelicans swooping, soft winds blowing, and the thin sparse traffic seemed to wave me on a journey that could have lasted forever and I wouldn't have cared.

Turning onto the main drag toward Mill Valley, I suddenly realized just how famished I was. Hunger gripped me like a long-lost friend, and I drove past my own street to the local stores of the little village I called home. I bought fresh fish, bread, wine, butter, milk, coffee, all the best things my body now cried out for. With two huge grocery bundles I walked quickly back to the car, smiling at everyone I hardly knew. My body felt light and energetic, filled with love and generosity to human and all other kind. Even the local cop got the biggest smile he'd had in weeks, as he awarded parking tickets to everyone except me.

Back in the house, the two Guatemalan cleaners got an unexpected bonus as their boss started cooking up a storm. I laid the table carefully as Nicki had always insisted, making my first celebration meal since she had died. With a big vase of flowers in the middle, I felt like a Rafael painting set perfectly in the center of a life that could have been attributed to the gods of pleasure and joy. My beautiful Nicki was back and had brought with her an adventure beyond my wildest dreams.

As I ate fully and drank rashly, I considered what all this could mean in the long term. For the first time since the whole adventure had begun, I gave thought to what it might all signify. What was she doing? Was she perhaps merely visiting to say goodbye, or did she intend to spend the rest of my life beside me, as would have been the case had she not contracted the cancer that had eaten her beautiful body? She had stood each time, in the apparitions, her beautiful sexy frame displayed before me in a way she had rarely done during her life. Her body was radiant, and the kiss that she planted on my head, and then today on my lips, had actually aroused me. Did she intend more of this? Would she come to our bed and make love with me, fire me up again, take me inside her, make love like some legendary goddess? Or was she merely playing with me, teasing me, another of her habits. During our times together, even after ten or more years, she would often tease me for days before allowing me entry to that place I loved so deeply. Was this her game? Was it a game at all? Where would it all go?

After exhausting my hunger, I sat by the door to the kitchen deck and gazed out at the deep blue of the skies, watched the trees blowing and bending toward one another, as though they echoed my questions and gave each other secret answers. The big crows and bluebirds darted about the land and scared off the cats that I had not seen for what seemed like days. I suddenly realized that I had not refreshed their food or water and they had probably imagined I was gone, departing as cats do to other food suppliers in the neighborhood. Quickly I put down several choices of fresh cat food from the expensive tins I had bought along with my own food, plus a big bowl of filtered water in their traditional places inside the open pantry. Two minutes later, as if by magic, they all three sauntered into the kitchen, greeted me without fuss and made their way to the bowls, delicately consuming in harmony until everything was gone. All four of us then moved upstairs to the main bedroom and collapsed on the huge bed, the three boys wrapped in each other like one huge cat, and I sprawled above them, forced into the minority position in one corner.

No one woke for hours until the front door-bell rang. I staggered down the stairs, bemused by too much alcohol and a shocked stomach working hard to digest the sudden input after three days of deprivation. Through the glass entrance I grunted to see Jennifer. She had to know, of course. She had to learn, I recalled. She would never give up, I capitulated, but then she was Nicki's best friend for more than twenty years — longer even than I had been. She was entitled, I allowed.

"Hi, Jen — thought you'd come sooner." She sidled into the large hallway looking a bit sheepish. "What's up?"

"I, er, I just wanted to see how you are." She paused. "I mean, did you really see Nicki?" She looked up into my eyes.

I was about to say "yes," but I stopped as Nicki stepped forward and stood at the top of the stairs.

She knew that Jennifer would not see her, and in a way it was the first time I really saw her myself, convincingly, in a way so that I could rely upon her continued presence. It was very personal in this respect, for she had transformed from a glancing ghost that floated and darted away from me like a humming bird, to being there, truly there.

What she had to give was for me alone, at least for now, but she wanted to motion me into silence. I was making rules for her that didn't truly apply. I went silent, looking from Jennifer to Nicki and back again. When it became clear that she could not see her, I became flustered and secretive and Jennifer detected the change.

"She's here now isn't she, in this room, right here? I know it, Gideon, I can tell." She started to look around in a vain attempt to sense Nicki's whereabouts and became flustered too and slightly angry at her inability, her disempowerment at our hands. Nicki motioned with her finger to her lips, indicating to me that she wanted her not to feel this way.

"Jen, this thing belongs to us still." I was tender with her, my voice low and calm, my gestures gentle. "Be patient. It might change. Please." I touched her arm, gently, and Jennifer let go of her questing, turning toward me. She opened her bag and pulled out two tapes, handing them to me.

"These are the only recordings of what happened on the ECG readings today and yesterday. I thought you should keep them here. There are some very curious people on campus. Better safe than sorry." She leaned forward, and kissed me on the cheek, moved to the door and left.

I turned to Nicki. "Can you stay like this, visible to me?" Nicki gestured that she could not. "Can you touch me again?" She motioned her hand into mine, and I felt the tingle of energy that moved between us as before. The three cats suddenly appeared from the upper floors, sat in that perfect cat position, licking fur, turning this way and that, completely in harmony with one another, and then all three looked directly up at Nicki and departed in unison as though they had come to check things out. Now that they knew all was going fine they could go about their business as usual. Nicki gently faded and was gone, but I knew now that she would be back.

# FOUR

I went to work in the usual way the following morning, trying to keep a normal balance in a life that had become distinctly abnormal. But I couldn't work. I could only twiddle my thumbs and look suspiciously at everyone as if they all knew what was happening and were suspicious of me. They weren't, of course. Nobody paid any mind to the earthquake stopping that Nicki and I had apparently performed. It had been forgotten and everyone had settled back into repairing the minor damage that had occurred, though I sensed there was some gossip going about related to Nicki's death and my strange behavior.

But I couldn't work, and soon realized that the real reason for this agitation in my heart was simple excitement that my long-loved Nicki was truly back in my life. This didn't really answer anything though, of course, because it made no sense at all "scientifically"; it gave me no rationale for my daily life. The delight of it hung there like a golden, sparkling mobile, set up for a fascinated innocent child who never questions flights of fancy. I was only just beginning to encounter my innocence at Nicki's hands. How could I believe and also experience something that was unbelievable, and extraordinary? And yet, as a scientist, how could I suspend my disbelief and simply live through it? Confusion, confusion, stay with the confusion, I told myself. This is what she might say in these circumstances.

I managed to escape from tapping my fingers on my desk, and speed home in Nicki's coupe. I found myself almost entirely without thought as I drove along the I-280 back toward the Richmond Bridge. Crossing through onto Highway 101, I felt more joy and freedom than I had ever experienced. Even when I was happy with Nicki I never felt this breathless delight. It was as though something holy had swept into my mind and body and cleared them out, leaving a sense of complete emptiness, complete lack of fear. I would have been happy if the drive had continued forever. In fact, even the idea of forever was absurd, for there was nothing I wanted more than simply to be doing what I was doing, whatever it was.

As I drove, thoughtless and filled with bliss, I managed to hit the right note for a moment. Each time a thought or an idea came into my mind, such as the notion of relaxing into confusion and not trying always to find answers — so conditions arrived in which this was possible. My lack of thought, a sort of natural state of meditation — had come to me from somewhere, from Nicki? It had arrived as though by request, by prayer, in answer — instantly. It seemed that Nicki was giving me constant small miracles of realization, opening me up to new ways of being.

Back home I opened the front door to be met by all three cats, sitting patiently ready for feeding time. They led me like a dutiful servant to their feeding area inside the pantry, and placed themselves perfectly by the bowls. I obeyed their commands, laying out lavish dishes of the best gourmet food for the boys who kept me company on cold lonely nights.

Then I went to the TV room and punched buttons aimlessly, still virtually without thought, and still in that same state of joyful simplicity. I spoke to Nicki, even though I did not know she was there.

"What have you done to me, Nicki?"

She did not reply.

"Have you made me something different? Have you made me special, or am I going crazy?" I paused. "I feel like I could do anything, make anything happen — miraculous yet simple things. It's exciting and frightening all at the same time. My heart feels like it will explode. Is this what you did when you kissed me?"

At that moment the sky lit up suddenly, with a bright ray of light, and the familiar Mill Valley winds began to blow outside. The trees rustled loudly and everything turned into a bright, sunny storm.

I stood up and went to the front porch, closing the door behind me to keep the cats from running into the falling night. The sudden light quickly turned into the dark of a heavy storm. The wind blew still more and everything took on the air of thunder. A huge strike of lightning blasted across the sky and thunder followed on its heels. I stood there, my hair blowing about my face, my whole body moving with the force of the gusts that raked the house. The wood beams in the roof cracked and groaned, while the trees echoed their sounds, whining and bending.

I lifted my arms into the air and embraced the stormy sky and the blustering winds with a kind of command, somehow joining with this reality in a way I had never experienced before — very unscientific, very deep inside me. And the wind obeyed my command, so suddenly that I almost fell backward as the force of it no longer supported me from behind. The storm died down immediately, the air stilled, and the fall of rain that had begun a moment before took over from the wind and gushed in heavy glorious billows.

I turned toward the front entrance, my heart thumping so hard that I felt slightly faint. Nicki stood close to me, supporting my soul with her own. Inside the house I fell to my knees and cried.

I was actually having fun with all this! I found myself able to reach out to him in ways I could not have predicted. Each new event, each profound new contact with him, each new empowerment, and reassurance for him — made me want to laugh. How could I possibly have done any of this during my life? With all its presentiments and apprehensions, life in the body offered too many blockages for this sort of behavior. And the greatest part was that it was all natural and complete in itself, always coinciding with his needs and his actions. I gave him of myself as I was after death, gift after gift. Maybe I could talk with him more. Maybe I could join with him more profoundly — even eventually give him some direct experience of my own world, not that I knew at all what that was, or where it was. But perhaps the very thought and the desire for that encounter would bring it about!

I went upstairs and sat on the sofa in the library, suddenly feeling very much alone. It was an unexpected sensation, but then I was beginning to realize that not only had my mind and my senses become more responsive — I could smell and see better, and my sense of taste had become much sharper in the last day or so, but also my emotions and moods were far more precise and exaggerated. It was as though everything in my body had suddenly grown in sensitivity to a point where my whole prior life seemed as though conducted in a fog. This feeling of aloneness was sharp and powerful and engulfed my whole body for a moment, leaving me weak and ready to cry again. I had been pouring out tears on a regular basis during the night and that morning — one reason I hesitated to go anywhere.

Rather than passing, my moodiness appeared to be growing. It was okay, but troublesome in a practical sense. Solutions were needed by that male mind, but they didn't come.

The telephone rang a couple of times in the next hour, but I didn't answer, allowing the Voicemail to pick up messages. I turned the ringer off. Much as this strange aloneness unsettled me, I wanted to perpetuate it. I wanted only to be with Nicki. I remained on the sofa, watching the darkness and stroking one of the cats. The other two snuck onto the end of the sofa and slept with me until Nicki came around again before dawn. As soon as she appeared the boys sat up, waking me instantly.

I sat bolt upright, and with a broad smile on my face, looked straight at her in the dark. I seemed able to see as well as though it were broad daylight.

I leaned forward as if to try to touch her, but received a gentle shock from the light aura that now surrounded her. "What's this, a guiding light?" The words tumbled out of my mouth, inconsequentially.

Nicki seemed happy that I had found my sense of humor again. "Yes, I guess it is. I don't really know what's happening to me, Gideon. My energy seems to change and grow."

"Are you afraid?" I could actually hear her — couldn't I? There was a voice there that presumably anyone else present would have been able to experience — or not? I couldn't be quite sure. Perhaps I heard her only in my heart. Her physical presence was real enough, after all. Her body was defined, at least in my eyes. There was no color, however, and she appeared to be dressed in a diaphanous garment that billowed like any self-respecting ghost would demand.

"Not exactly. I'm sort of bewildered." She sat down where the cats had vacated the sofa, and turned toward me. I leaned backward and positioned two pillows to rest against.

"How about you?"

"Bewildered would be a good word, but totally calm nevertheless, at least right now. I feel like everything has suddenly come alive for the first time. I've never felt like this. I wonder sometimes when it will all end, but apart from that there's much less fear than before. It's just wonderful as it is, somehow, except for the mood swings."

"What do you expect to happen?" Nicki asked.

"Happen? It'll all stop, I imagine."

"And what will you do then?"

"Continue to be in love with you. Why are you so glowing? What's happening to you? Are you becoming an angel?"

She laughed. "That's just a word I suppose. It doesn't mean anything to me now. I imagine there must be angels for angel-dreamers — Christians and so on. Kind of feels like nonsense, except." She stopped, as though something important had occurred to her.

"But I want to know — won't you tell me?" I pressed her gently. "I mean, simple things. How do we talk together? How come you're here? What am I looking at? Where do you live — you know — things like that — stuff?" Still she remained silent, and her image faded slightly again. "What's happening? You look like you figured something out."

"I can't tell you yet — I don't know anything for sure. I get moments when I feel like there's some sense to what's happening, but then it disappears again, like just now. It's almost as though when you ask me things I begin to feel some certainty, some sense of truth about what's happening to me, as though you ground me by asking things." I looked happy, as she told me this. "You'll find out what you need to know soon enough, my love. It's not that I *could* tell and won't. It is that I don't know myself. Here, where I am, across this veil from you, things don't work through the mind. It's why I gave you the gift I did, emptying your mind so you could feel me more easily. I didn't know when I did it, but I can see now what I did and the consequences of it. This is how it works. Things unfold here, they get released through us."

"Us?" I perked up.

"There are many like me, though I've never met any of them. But I know they exist. I'll meet them in a different way, a different time — when I need to I guess, though that need hasn't really arisen yet because I'm so concentrated on you. But I know that there's more to come — more encounter, more relatives you might say!"

"Are there others like me who meet others like you?" I sat up straight.

"Perhaps, I don't know."

"You release small bits of information to me, drip by drip."

"It's the only way I know how. I can only answer questions as they come. There's no cumulative memory or thought process. I can tell you only that I exist so close to you that I'm part of you. We are not separated except by your concept of death and time. The veil between us is only a veil because of your conditioning — nothing else. When you die you will pass through that veil, and we will be together again in the same body, as one. That's the nearest I can get to explaining it and I'm not even very sure of that." She shifted her body gently on the sofa, and I wondered where these motions arose form. Was she experiencing physical sensations, or were they simply habits not yet abandoned?

"You mean, like two realms of existence?"

"No — there are no different realms, only the same realm — one world, one universe, one place. We both exist in it. The only thing that separates us is your thoughts and the thinker you create behind them. You are separated only by your idea that you're separated. The thinker is created by the thought and the thought by the thinker. You create them both, and all they do is take us apart."

"Difficult." I looked out of the window, hearing a gentle rain.

"And unimportant also, for the moment. Forget about it. There will be more of what you call miracles. In fact, none of the events so far are miracles really, they're just normal things that you can't see from where you are."

"More earthquakes?"

"I doubt it. I don't know — but for sure other things that you won't expect."

"But what about...I don't know...what about where you live? How do you live? What's it like? Is it cold and warm, are their seasons, places to go, flowers and trees like here?"

"Could be. In fact, as you say those things they appear for me, but I'm still very much attached to you and where you are, and to where I was. I'm still there in a way. Still living with you in the place I always did. Everything that I want for you happens through me into you and you into me, I guess."

"Say more please — say more. Just keep talking to me. It's so wonderful to hear you tell me things, just like you used to do, remember?"

"Yes, I remember. We used to tell each other everything."

"That was one of the most painful things after you left. It was so very hard not to hear what had happened to you. Why you decided to finish it all. I was so angry and so hurt. For a while there I hated you for depriving me of you." I started to cry again. She put her hand forward, and I felt it brush away the tears.

"One thing I can tell you, here I've learned never to drag the past into the present to bring pain to ourselves or others. It's worthless." Her hand drifted through mine and rested on my lap comfortingly. I reached out to lay mine upon it and once again felt that eerie and glorious tingle of energy.

"But the past means so much." I wanted to rub against the vision of her ghostly hand to get more of her, but she withdrew slightly, as though this drained her. Perhaps, I thought, my sadness and dragging of the past, as she put it, brought this sadness also to her. And of course it did. There were tears in her eyes too.

"There is no past, Gideon. There has never been a past and there never will be a past. There is no future either. There never has been and there never will be. There is only now." Nicki moved her hands in a kind of French gesture of emphasis. Her head turned toward the window as though she saw something, but quickly snapped back to hold me in her concentrated stare.

"This moment now — nothing else whatever. When you bring up your memories of what you see as your past life, all you do is experience, in this moment.

If you perpetuate that memory then it is there with you now, and now, and now. When you bring up memories to hurt you or others, all you do is make a new moment. It has nothing whatsoever to do with the experience you had at the time you call the past — absolutely nothing."

When she spoke, the concepts seemed to enter me through somewhere other than my ears or my mind. The message arrived through my heart and literally changed my whole being in that moment. I understood her on a completely unfamiliar level. I fell silent. The sadness evaporated, but quickly my mind returned. Tell me more, tell me more, it echoed silently. And of course, as I slouched further and further down into the padding of the sofa, she did.

"Think of it this way. If you constantly live somewhere else — in England or India or Italy — you are not being here in California. Likewise, if you live somewhere else in your mind or in time, you are not being in this moment. You become so preoccupied by the fantasy of the past or future, that you miss what's going on right now." She paused. I breathed more quickly. "What's happening between us is so real and so simple. We're together again — I say "again," but we were never separated. Delight in it. I do. It's absolutely wonderful because I can tell you everything. I can say how sorry I am that I hurt you. I can tell you how much I acted out of what I thought was love, not anything else. I can smooth your life with my mini-miracles. I can treat you better than I ever treated you during our lives together. Maybe I can even take you and bring you to my world, though I don't really know yet what that means." My mouth was already hanging open during her whole monologue, but this possibility was incredible beyond my wildest dreams.

"Really? My God — how could that be?"

"Don't get too excited — I don't know what might be possible, but what I notice is that here, desires, or prayers, or what you call thoughts, or notions, seem always to bring some kind of action after they occur."

"Yes, yes." I was getting so excited I could hardly contain myself. "I noticed that too, today, while I was driving back from the lab. Somehow things seemed always to coincide with a notion. I'd have a thought and suddenly it was happening."

"Yes, and sometimes I wonder if we're so close still that these notions and thoughts occur in each of us at the same time, as though we too were coinciding with life, or existence, or whatever." She grew somehow fainter — her presence wavering slightly.

I turned my head as she disappeared from sight, and I slept. There had been no more to be said in that instance, and so it came to an end. The night passed soundlessly for me, my sleep the sleep of angels, my dreams unheard, and my mind silent.

# FIVE

I woke early as usual. I stretched out my hand and felt the soft thick fur of Tashy. Purring started instantly and I opened my eyes to see him unfolding coyly across the sheets. Somehow I had moved from the library sofa to the bed during the night. I couldn't remember when or why. The blinds were open, and the sun shone across my face with blinding light. I was sweating slightly from the heat, and the memory of talking with Nicki was still in the front of my mind, as though it had occupied my dreams also. But she was not there, of course. I was also naked, which I hadn't been last night. Had I undressed myself or had Nicki done more of her magic?

I stroked the cat for a while and then sat up in bed, checking out my body for signs of anything else I might have forgotten. Everything seemed in place, and reaching out for the glass of stale water beside the bed, I touched the stem of the lamp and got a static shock from the metal.

"What's going on, Tashy?" The cat perked up at the sudden movement, ready to run from his unpredictable master. I ventured to touch the metal again, my other hand lazily rubbing Tashy's belly. The shock was greater this time and the poor animal jumped a foot in the air and sped out of the room. His hair stood up along his spine and the back of his neck, though I only caught a brief glimpse of his departing body.

I went into the bathroom and stood in front of the mirror, my face breaking into a smile as I saw that every hair on my head was up like a porcupine's bristles.

"Uh oh, what now?!" I took a comb and tried to bring my unruly hair into order, but the static prevailed, so I turned on the shower, and waiting for the temperature to rise, I kept plastering at the hair in an attempt to regain my personal dignity. It was quite nice, in a way, I thought, not to have to worry about what someone else might think of my appearance.

There was this too, sometimes. When you've been so long with someone intensely close, gone through all the experiences that occur between two people — good, bad, difficult, easy — there is that relief; that freedom on occasion when the lover is absent, though when they're gone in death it's different, of course. When your lover simply takes a back seat in your life with a long trip or even a separation, it's different because somewhere there is still that hope or knowledge that things will return to normal. We cling so tightly to love relationships. The morphic fields of love and hate bind us so tightly; chemically, psychologically, and even when the bond is broken through anger and the conditioning that brings on pain, we still try to bind up the water parcel with string. We never want to leave and be gone completely when life is still there. But with death, at least I thought so, there is an end to it. There is a permanence where the heart and soul and, more important, the body, must make amends with the past and move on. But could I? Could I move on in this case?

When a couple blows it; when they caste their nets in different waters because life takes that new turn, there are the barriers and protectors of anger and hate to help facilitate separation. In death, the one that is left behind finds mostly the good things to dote on.

But for me she was still here. She had not departed and left me free to encounter my life alone. She haunted me now, literally, and in these simple moments, like standing before a mirror with my hair awry, and my aging body strange to me, I could at least relax in that simple, foolish moment, and enjoy myself for once, unequivocally. Except it couldn't be allowed to last — this freedom.

The day after I had sat with Gideon in the library of our house, I became aware of someone I had never seen before — a young woman with a beautiful exotic name. She was called Ansinoé, and for some reason I could not explain, she became significant to me, even though Gideon had not met her either. It seemed so strange to me to have this person appear on the horizon without warning, as though I possessed some ethereal radar that detected presences and feelings, even though there was not physicality to my witnessing. I knew about her more quickly than he did, though I had no idea why, to begin with, but then, as I asked the question, it became clear that her place would be a significant one in the story. She was interested in my man! He was still my man — that too brought implications into my heart and mind. She was pretty after all — think about this. She was younger even than I had been. I was still his only lover, even in my ethereal state, for I had not left him since death — at least insofar as I could tell.

As I became able to see her, appearing somehow out of a mist of absence, Ansinoé sat making an album of pictures she had taken of him. The photography was mostly of Gideon going in and out of the faculty offices at Berkeley — Ansinoé knew this place well. As I read her thoughts it became clear that this had been her campus as his student these last three years. She had spied on him, and was quite sure he never noticed her interest during the lectures she attended as part of her post-graduate course. There was one good portrait that she had taken of him in his home with a long-distance lens. She had felt guilty doing it, but it was also exciting. She was like a voyeur or a journalist, sneaking up on his privacy in our home in Mill Valley and snapping the shot as he sat in the window of what appeared to her a library. It had been the day that I had sat with him on that sofa and answered his questions.

Ansinoé studied the picture of the side of his head above a windowsill. Taking a magnifying glass she looked closely at the pixilated photograph, as she had noticed a kind of shadow next to it, to the left of his head. She couldn't make out what it signified but it gave her a slight chill. She tagged the picture and wrote, "enhance and clarify," on the yellow tag, then tucked it into a buff envelope and set it aside for the lab.

I could see, watching this girl from my vantage point beyond the veil, that something about Gideon made her feel protective of him. She knew that this quest of hers was crazy and obsessive, but she justified it as necessary for her thesis on paranormal activities. Everyone in the faculty had singled him out as the most likely candidate for such a work, given the rumors that he had seen a ghost of his departed wife and his work in the department of paranormal research. She reassured herself that once the research was completed she would take it to him first and never show it to anyone else, and that he would forgive her the small faux pas of spying on him. In any case, she could always censor the parts of her research that might upset him.

She would not suck on him as journalists often do. She would not disturb his grief or add to his pain. Perhaps she might even help him by coming up with information that would make his contact with his wife easier.

How strange it was for me to see all this happening, for in bringing her into my consciousness I could see events in her past. It was as though I had captured a radio broadcast that drifted through the universal consciousness being broadcast for my benefit. Once again, these perceptions taught me the nature of existence beyond the veil. Ask the question, and the answer is given in all its perfect detail. I considered if perhaps I would be able to do this with anyone I wished — my parents, my grandparents — all that had become trimmed into neat little packages of memory and recognition.

Ansinoé had heard much talk on campus, and I could hear the echoes of it as she reconsidered her research, adding everything up in her mind to make the result she wished to achieve — contact with my husband.

"He just stood there in his office and yelled 'stop' at the top of his voice. We all heard it, and the earthquake obeyed him," the student told her.

No matter that nobody was actually in his office when he said it — details of that kind were not the task of gossips. Whether he actually stopped an earthquake or not wasn't really the point. Whether his wife had returned after death or not didn't honestly matter. These things weren't made of fact, but theory, and he was so goddam cute after all.

She pulled the enigmatic picture out of the buff envelope again and looked once more at the weird shadow next to his face for a moment and then slipped it back in. I watched her and knew in that instant that she would make a significant discovery that would affect us all.

She had heard talk of concern among students and teachers, that the Dean was angry about the "disturbances" caused by Gideon's strange behavior. The general sense that she got was that no one really believed in any "powers" or discoveries that Gideon might have achieved. His subsequent retreat to his home, and refusal to speak with anyone, compounded the debate so that the whole thing had grown into a kind of sideshow. Faculty members seemed worried for him:

"He was popular before this happened, and we still love him, but he's head of the department of phenomenology, you know. It's a tough job proving ghosts are real. Some people think maybe he's got a bias that might have driven him to make all this up."

"All what up?" Ansinoé, gossiping, had asked one of his faculty students.

"Just the stuff about his wife. I'm not supposed to say. The poor guy needs some space to recover after all." The girl edged away from Ansinoé.

"There's talk that his wife haunts him, and that he saw her during that earthquake, right? Is that what you mean?"

"Yes, sort of, it's the death, yes?" But Ansinoé had seen in the girl's eyes that it wasn't the death, but maybe what had come after it.

Ansinoé had returned to the students' hall, where she started sifting through the faculty notes that followed all experiments on paranormal activity taking place on the university machinery. It felt to her like a worthy case. The poor man needed her protection, at least her concern perhaps. She found no copy tapes of any equipment recordings, which must have meant he had taken them home. This increased her interest.

What would she do with all this, I wondered? How would this bring him into her arms?

She turned on the small TV and flicked through the Network news channels for anything interesting. There was nothing, of course, and Ansinoé clicked the TV off in disgust.

She had thought, at the time when Gideon supposedly stopped the earthquake, that it was as well that none of the local press had picked up the rumors. Secretly, somewhere inside her, she wished they had, because then she could have been his protector and find a simple way into his life.

I could feel that all this was more of an excuse for her growing emotional attraction to him, and that ultimately I would have to watch him become involved with her. How did it feel to me? I tried not to feel too much, following my own advice to allow matters to remain in the present, though what passed for my heart did not like it.

For Ansinoé, once she had heard about Gideon's loss, it seemed most likely that he was playing out some deep devastation in his life, though this, of course, did not lessen the possibility that he possessed special psychic powers released by his tragedy. Her heart swelled as she thought more about it. In her research into social phenomenology, she had found many cases in which major life-change initiated this inceptive phase. Miracle-making, in itself a rare ability, was most commonly associated with loss or crisis.

Ansinoé had an intense desire for examples of extreme consciousness in unique human beings. She hoped that perhaps this Gideon Falwall might be an example of that uniqueness. She hoped that if he was, she would be allowed to discover it.

There had been much talk among graduate students and faculty about him locking himself away in his house, never even walking down to the mailbox. She had been there and checked it to see that it was overflowing with several days' mail. He didn't need visitors, obviously, and certainly not one who had selfish intentions. She decided to wait and try to find a way to make contact once he emerged into the world again.

I watched her place the folder and envelope neatly into her briefcase, close it up, and leave for her home in Belvedere. She would sit on the deck of her house, she thought, and watch the boats go by — try to forget about those selfish motives. Perhaps she'd take her Uncle Doring's boat out.

In hearing this thought from her mind I could instantly see everything she owned. It was fascinating, like a magic show: a whole picture of her home, her past life, her uncle, his boat, the deck, everything that surrounded her and made her feel secure. I could see her childhood, lonely and remote from everyone in her family, the death of her parents, the dreadful and intense fear she had felt since then, and at last, of course, how all this lead inevitably toward Gideon, and even me, the all-seeing ghost who spied upon her. It was incredible, like a tapestry suddenly laid out before me, visually, sensually, with all the memories, the doubts and fears, the emotions, everything I could possibly need to know about her. And the motivation for all this was the most significant aspect of it. I wanted to know because I wanted to feel who she was. Here was the source of this magnificent conjuring trick in the parlor of my existence.

Half an hour later, she turned into the generous driveway of the home she had inherited from the man who had been her only real experience of a father. The house was nestled generously in a one-acre plot between two other homes right on the waterfront. Belvedere always felt to her like a perfect haven, and she had spent most of her childhood in this home with Uncle Doring before he eventually died of his excessive interest in alcohol.

I could see on this broad vista of her memory that he had never been violent, however, though a little crotchety sometimes. It seemed that the drink only really calmed him from all the pressure he had always undertaken working for the British Foreign Service. Not that Ansinoé knew much about what he actually did, only that it took him away from home often, to foreign places — Kosovo, Afghanistan, Belarus, Russia — places where Uncle Doring needed to drink just to be welcome among the people he worked with. He would never actually tell her anything after one of his two-month-long trips, except that he was exhausted, and that he had missed her and loved her like a daughter.

In that moment, as I listened to her memories that lay about her mind like snow flakes, I could see that older man's face when he would arrive crumpled after a trip, and gradually, over a few days, settle into that warm absolution which seemed to come from a mixture of sleep and alcohol. I could see him, from my place in "heaven," as a good man who never actually managed to enter human flesh successfully. So many there were like him. And as his memory occurred for her, so it occurred for me, and briefly he brushed my arm in his own spirit form, and sent messages to her through my presence — as though I were a psychic in touch with the living.

The house always welcomed her even when he was absent. As a child, during his times away Uncle

Doring had appointed a warm-hearted child-minder to smile at her home-coming after school each day. When she was a young adult, it always seemed like Uncle Doring was still there in the house when she swung into the drive in the huge Range Rover he kept for her use.

Now it still felt the same, and I could see that Uncle Doring's spirit continued to watch over her, though he had not chosen to develop the contact that I had with Gideon, preferring to remain in the background and only "visible" to her in more subtle ways of comfort and protection. Did all spirits do this? Were we all present in the lives of our loved ones? So it seemed to me in that moment of realization.

She lived happily alone, in a kind of calm warm coziness, never really interrupted by the troubles of the outside world.

Ansinoé brought the supermarket packages into the front entrance and dumped everything on the kitchen table, leaving the front door open so that her cat, Kadabra, could run in and out instead of having to squeeze her way through the cat-door. As though on cue, this extraordinary cat swayed into the kitchen, leapt with surprising agility onto the stove top, and curled up, purring her welcome. Ansinoé thought this was Uncle Doring in a perfect disguise, though actually, I could see that the cat had its own spirit. For a moment Uncle Doring stood close by them both, still watching over his niece, apparently unaware of my presence. What was this spirit world I lived in? There was still so much for me to learn.

Kadabra had been born the very day that Uncle Doring had died, and her favorite treat was a small brandy and milk. How human presences remain, couched in the subtlety of ghosts, prolonged in the complexity of the spirit.

The messages on her Voicemail could wait, for no one knew that she was home yet, so there was time for rest before beginning her full-moon rituals. She lit the ready-made open fire, turned on the huge digital TV in the living room, and punched the stereo button that would play her "hit-list" of music videos on the screen. Pressing another small button on the remote control she placed a small inset picture of CNN on one corner of the screen, and then another of Channel 4 news on the other corner. This way she could relax, and with the occasional glance at the text-overlay she could stay in touch with any news items of interest.

I watched as Ansinoé, unloading the contents of the bag into the refrigerator, considered again the picture of Gideon sitting inside his home just a few miles away. Something about the fact that he was so near made her feel warm inside, and yet the oblique shadow image on the photograph gave her sense of well-being a twinge of doubt. She closed the freezer door on the packages of fish and meat and once again took the picture from its envelope. At the last moment she had not left it for processing by the lab, thinking that maybe she would get some ideas from further examination of it herself.

Taking it to her home office, she turned on the computer and the scanner and placed the image face down on the surface of the glass. When the computer was ready, she opened the scanner software so that she'd have a high enlargement capability. Returning to the kitchen while the long scanning process completed, she cut some fresh bread and prepared a sandwich. She poured a beer and gathered up the huge sandwich onto an ornate glass dish, moving back to the home office. The scanning was just done.

I could feel her enthusiasm and youth and loved her in that instant. She would be good for Gideon, oh, how good she would be.

She diverted the image to the huge TV screen in the living room, took in her food and drink, and sat close to the screen so that she could clearly see the five-foot-wide image of Gideon's head and shoulders and the strange enigmatic shadow to his left.

At first she studied his expression. The shot was much improved by the scanning but it was still hard to make out his expression. She reduced the image so that details became more visible. His face spoke of what appeared to be pleasure. He was smiling and his eyes were soft, warmed by whatever he saw or felt. He was a handsome man with a depth of compassion and joy in his expression. It looked as though he was in the presence of something exceptional, something, well, very special. I could see and feel — her discovery, and the turn of her mind and heart toward him grew more focused. I could sense the fields of energy about her body intensifying. So incredible, this new discovery of mine, so wonderfully incredible.

Ansinoé turned her attention to the shadow and further reduced the image on the screen to see if she could make sense of it. It was a little like examining an Expressionist painting at close quarters, a Degas between the eyes. She took another gulp of the beer and was about to bite again into the sandwich when she stopped in mid movement. Standing up, Ansinoé stepped back a foot in the realization of what she saw. She had to place the plate of food down onto the floor as she almost upturned the beer.

The shadow was of my head, shoulders, and torso down to the waist. And yet it wasn't a straightforward photograph, but a vague double-image that appeared as though it floated in midair. Unlike the image of Gideon, this aspect of the photograph was transparent. She could see through it to a painting, on the wall behind. It had been this painting that had confused the shadowy image of the photograph, and although she could not make out the picture, she could now see that the shadowy image on the print was of a woman with long dark hair and what seemed like naked shoulders. It was an image of me, almost lost in the absence of life, but still visible in the imagination of hope.

Shocked and excited, Ansinoé ignored the fact that Kadabra was devouring her sandwich. Darting back into her office, she rescanned the image even more precisely and sat there, by now a touch intoxicated. Finally, after almost twenty minutes, she flashed it onto the TV screen. Centering onto the shadow she confirmed her diagnosis. Kadabra had by now collapsed onto the rug by the open fire and was snoring off her excesses, oblivious of her mistress's intense excitement. This was the image of a woman, except that she was transparent!

Thus I watched my husband's future lover. What more could I do but stand aside and take it all in. I could not even wait for it to happen. So much had been revealed to me, too. As this young woman found evidence of my ghostly presence in Gideon's life, so I found evidence of the presence of other spirits in my life beyond the veil. Once again, in that moment of realization, there came the manifestation of it. Thousands, hundreds of thousands of spirits suddenly converged about me, touching me. Millions of souls, billions of characters, beings, creatures, all merged in a vast, infinite existence of past lives still living in the spirit world. In this moment of emotional truth, this extraordinary, slight distancing from my dearly beloved husband, I came home for a moment. In the knowledge that he was about to enter into another romantic connection within his life, I found evidence of my own life after death.

# SIX

One of the calls recorded on my Voicemail from the previous day was from someone called Ansinoé which in her own voice sounded "ansinoay," and didn't strike me as being particularly significant, except that she had a rather nice voice. There were six other messages from Jennifer, but I figured they could go into the wait-and-see for the moment. I would call her anyway, later. It was, in fact, too late at night to return this Ansinoé's call.

I told Nicki of this moment as we talked when she visited me, for this moment signified beyond all other moments in my mind. It was the beginning of an end, and a new beginning. It separated our hearts and yet joined them for all time. It brought our bodies apart, for we would never again physically meet in the old form, though we had hoped for it. Yet it sealed our togetherness for infinity, though neither of us knew it at that moment.

I think sometimes, when I see Nicki's drifting heart, that if I had answered the phone to Ansinoé that night I might have done something differently, but in retrospect this is no more than a fantasy, like the phantasm of talking with Nicki each time she comes. I am destined to wonder forever hoping for her, never truly touching, never really embracing, but always knowing where she is in her fatal world, while I remain in mine on the other side of the veil.

I watched his confusion in these moments of change. It was like watching a child grow up so rapidly that he has no time to adapt to the lanky body overtaking the muscles. He floundered at every turn, and yet he always covered up his softness and insecurity with that innate and characteristic brusqueness. To be so strong and not know it, to be so sensitive and English and yet unable to let it out to anyone — not even me now, especially these times, for I could not be there for him always as I had been when in the body.

So often I wished I could remain constantly by his side to guide him through the changes, but then I didn't really know what the changes were myself, except as they happened, and then without any understanding of why they were happening, at least, not in ways that I could reveal to him. It wasn't that there were rules that I had to play by. There were just things I could see but could not tell him, could not open my mouth and reveal them to him. I got hints, though, as when Ansinoé's message was left on his Voicemail. I knew what was important and what wasn't, but I could not have told him what would come of that message, who that person was to be in his changing condition, nor who would be the lover and the friend, the helpers and the enemies. I was never privy to the future nor to the motivations, except through some immediate instinct. All I ever knew for sure was that it was all for the good — that everything was always for the good.

The receptionist was just like all other hospital portals, painted with a red line across her mouth, while the rest was green.

"Yes?"

"I have an appointment with Dr. Bauer." I felt important, though I didn't know why.

"Please take a seat." She bartered.

"Where shall I take it?" I tried, knowing that displaying a sense of humor in America, especially in California, was much like trying to float an octopus, all arms and legs and no grin.

I remained leaning against the counter, overtime. She still didn't look up, but attended to a black woman with a huge child, whom she berated for not having the right paperwork. I stared but they both ignored me. I sauntered away and bumped into a woman who introduced herself as Dr. Bauer. She took my arm and led me away as though I had just won the Nobel Prize.

My strange "enlivened" condition, which I imagined had been brought about by Nicki's returned presence in my life, had produced some wonderful pluses, but also some rather disturbing negatives. Since the day of the kiss and the earthquake, my whole body felt like it belonged to someone else. I had become hugely energetic and enormously excited, with bouts of great emotional uncertainty followed rapidly with a renewed sense of life as the source of joy and happiness. My attitude to everything around me had become somehow "enlightened," as though I was seeing everything for the first time — the color of light, the presence of green in the undergrowth, the constant beauty of my surroundings, the intimacy I seemed to have developed with nature around my house. But with all this glorious exegesis there were also terrible headaches. I would wake in the middle of the night, and my head would pound and grunt at me until I got up out of bed and permitted the brain to settle its discomfort. Dr. Bauer had been recommended to me by Jennifer, and here I was for what I hoped would be a useful consultation.

"Come to my office. Jennifer tells me you need help. We're old friends, and she's concerned about you." She nuzzled my arm with her breast and I wondered what variety of bra would make it feel so firm and solid. Nicki had never explained that sort of thing to me.

"Thank you. What did she say?" I was not serious about my condition, but Dr. Bauer looked deeply into my eyes as I spoke. She sat me down and scuttled round the other side of her desk, as though conscious that she should take up her position of authority before passing judgment on my body.

"Something about your loss, and headaches? She wasn't very specific." She let out a long sigh. "So tell me?"

"My wife died, and I have terrible headaches."

"Okay, sounds reasonable, so let's take a few tests first, and we can see what's maybe going on." She was muscular, quite short, and with an hourglass figure. Her stethoscope was slung about her neck at random, as though she didn't care whose heart beat into it, and her hair was slightly mussed, probably from a long day's night. She smiled, and I noticed a missing tooth on one side of her upper jaw. I wondered vaguely if someone had punched her.

She needled me, pinched me, made me give samples in plastic containers. She breathed with me, squeezed my testicles, pumped my chest, and constricted my blood. She heard my heart and sniffed my breath, pocked my eyes and furrowed my brow. She narrowed my eardrums, scurried my nostrils, wracked my brains, then left me alone for an hour and a half.

Suitably en-doctored I remained patient. Entirely invaded I felt okay. She was, in my opinion, a good doctor, for despite all that she embarked upon my body, I still felt good about hers.

Upon her return to my waiting room, she sat again and shuffled her notes. She seemed hesitant in her diagnosis.

"I specialize, as it happens, in the human processes of aging, though my work is not what you might consider regular medical practice but largely related to certain aspects of Chinese medicine. That's my work outside this clinic, and although I need to run more detailed tests, it seems that you are aging very slightly more slowly than normal, though it's quite hard to define what's normal in these cases, particularly in someone I have only looked at once." She paused for breath.

"There've been a series of discoveries recently on aging where geneticists have created races of super organisms — fruit flies, for instance, that can live double their natural lifespan. Other labs have bred mice that spontaneously regenerate parts of their bodies. Quite dramatic stuff really." She paused again, and I wondered if she was going to tell me more about the fruit flies. She looked at me, and I looked back. My mind was turgid, uncertain. What was she telling me this for? Had she found a cure for aging? Did I care?

"Er," I said. "And?" I said. "Can you tell this, as you say, from one visit?"

"Technically no, not for sure at this point, but I've learned from my experiments with animals and insects that there are signs of a slowing down of aging that are evidenced by particular symptoms that you appear to have, such as very low blood pressure, normal pulse rates, and the presence of certain levels of activity in the brain. Your blood pressure is ninety over fifty. Under normal circumstances that would make your ability to function normally almost impossible, yet your pulse is okay and you're not showing any signs of anemia.

"Gideon, it appears that you may have developed some unusual form of natural age retardant. Your body seems to have learned a way to slow down your aging process. As a result you may live longer than normal. I cannot, at this point, tell you exactly what this will mean, but your physical condition is, well, that of a younger man."

"Really?" I gawped.

"Pretty much, subject to further tests."

"Nicki." I said.

"What?" Dr. Bauer moved away from her chair and sat on the edge of the desk next to me, as though she either wanted to hear more clearly or she was practicing some therapeutic stance taught to her in Med-school.

"Doesn't matter, I understand. Is there any problem, I mean, what about the headaches?" I didn't look at her. I was already rehearsing what I would say when I saw Nicki again ("What have you done? What do you want me to do with all this life? Why couldn't you shorten it instead of extending it? Are you nuts?

Which miracle is this one? Where the hell am I?" Et cetera.)

"I'll have preliminary test results in a few days, at least for the present round. They'll tell us the likelihood of your life span being more than normal, and the problems if any. The headaches are probably a reaction to your recent loss. Or perhaps something to do with this slowing of the aging process, which appears to be a fairly recent change."

"Really — how do you know that? You have my medical records? But I'm an Englishman."

"You mean Englishmen don't have medical records?" She giggled.

"Hah, right, I guess it's all on computer now?"

"Yes, everything's on computer now. Your records were registered when you got your green card. There was no evident sign of these physical conditions then. It seems to have started in the past few weeks. We can also tell from the formation of the new cells how recent they are. Might have something to do also with the loss of your wife."

"You could say that." I muffled my mouth with the back of my hand for some reason, perhaps trying to act normally.

"Well, maybe that could cause it. I'll be in touch — maybe come to your house on a visit with Jennifer some time, if that's okay. Oh, and it's probably better that you keep this to yourself." She stood up, now distracted — onto the next patient.

"Thanks. Please, visit anytime you wish." I moved toward her and for some reason I didn't really understand, I took her shoulders and kissed her once on each cheek. She blushed. I left, feeling distinctly European.

What would he do with this? How could I soften the blow? Why was it happening? I couldn't answer any of these questions as I watched him hesitate in the doctor's room. He staggered slightly as though he would lose his balance, and he leaned against the desk with one hand to steady himself. The doctor put her hand on his shoulder and comforted him with soft words, as though she had told him that he was going to die sooner rather than later. And yet, like me, he knew it was right, that the kiss I had laid upon his forehead had changed something in his body and mind. In this quintessential moment the reason for my charmed kiss seemed apparent. It had set in motion a progress beyond the rational, a wing of change that might lead anywhere from the physical into the metaphysical. Existence offered perfection, after all, though unrecognized.

Once home I locked the doors of the house, checked that all the blinds and drapes were down, turned on all the lights, and sat in the library.

"Nicki? Come, Nicki, tell me about this thing. You know I'm not good alone." I muttered like this for about an hour, but Nicki stayed away.

Then I remembered the message on my Voicemail from a woman named Ansinoé. I went back and listened to it, searching for reassurance, just for something to do, to divert my sense of inner panic.

"Hi, Gideon, I'm Ansinoé. You probably don't remember me. I'm a student and attend some of your lectures. I need to speak with you. I'm not a journalist. Please call me. It's a matter of great importance." And a number. I called. She did not answer for ages, and then her voice sounded as though it were a message on a machine. I breathed deeply and prepared in my mind what I would record.

"Hi, I'm Gideon Falwall. I have your message...."

"Yes, Gideon."

I jumped. It was a human being. "Ahhh, okay, I thought...."

"I know. My friends do that. They think I'm a machine."

"Yes." I hesitated. Was she psychic, or was I stupid?

"I'm a bit psychic, sorry." She said. I worried, was my longer life going to be like this?

"What did you want?" I decided to get right to the point.

"I need to speak with you." She offered, again.

"You're not a journalist, right? I don't want to speak with journalists. They upset everything."

"I agree. No. I'm not a journalist, as I said, I'm a student in your department. I'm also okay really. I won't hurt you." It sounded good to me. I believed her, and as I listened and believed, Nicki appeared for a split second, like a subliminal advertising campaign, and nodded approval.

"Okay, come and see me. Come here. You know where here is?"

"Yes."

"Tomorrow?" How did she know where I lived? What the hell?

"Okay." I hung up.

As I let go of the receiver, Nicki appeared.

"So . . . " She sounded like a wife who has discovered a poorly guarded secret.

"What?" I shrugged, not knowing what I had done wrong but knowing that I had.

"Changes happening, maybe big changes." She settled down on the bed, then stood again as though slightly at a loss. She drifted into the library and took up her customary position curled up on the sofa. I thought, where is she sitting right now? Is there a sofa in her realm of existence?

"Oh, dear, sounds serious, what's happening?" I sat beside her, but she did not touch me.

"I don't really know. But something is changing. I've found a place to take you."

"Really? Where? On the other side?"

"Yes. On the other side."

"Will it be soon?"

"I don't know when or where truly. Just that it is being made to happen."

She knew as she said this, I learned later, that what she was doing was actually a provision, a sort of device, something crafted for a purpose, though she could not admit to this because she didn't as yet know what it meant or why she was doing it. She knew in her soul, though, that now she had learned that everything we can do in the life of the flesh can also occur in the life of the soul, her life was as good and as bad as mine.

"Don't go without me." I quipped, hoping to allay any anxiety I imagined she felt. She merely smiled, reached out, and touched my forehead and allowed her hand to slide gently down my cheek. Then she vanished, leaving me wholly unsatisfied and not a little flustered.

What could I say to him? How could I transport doubts in my own heart into his? Why would I want to burden him with something that wasn't yet even known to him? This woman, this Ansinoé, what would she be to him? I couldn't prevent it, for I did not want to. It was a part of our change, our gentle, natural drifting apart. Had I been alive and in my body, I would simply have made sure that he did not need or wish to be joined with another. I would have made scenes, no doubt, acted unreasonably out of my feminine consciousness. I might have ranted and raved and acted with vengeance. But I was not in my body, and I knew that none of this meant anything to us — that our togetherness was always to be the same in each present we occupied. But still, I hurt, for still I knew that he would take his leave from me in this way. Life moved on. I had departed from him, and existence would provide his entertainment and his fulfillment in other forms I could not create. This was, after all, part of his departing grief.

The following morning Jennifer called four more times. Soon Ansinoé would arrive. I hoped that Jennifer would not appear while this Ansinoé was visiting. She would get the wrong idea for sure, but I didn't want to call her yet. Nicki didn't reappear, and I wondered why she was only popping in with advice and warnings, expressions of help and then instant disappearances. What the hell was all that about? Everything seemed to be happening in double-time. The doorbell rang.

"Hi. I'm Ansinoé." She was tall, pretty, very young, slightly gawky, smiling. She could have been a Jehovah's Witness, but they would not have sent her out on such an errand. She could have been Jewish, but they would have kept her at home — loved her, spoiled her, brushed her long dark hair. She was intensely haired, on her head like a mane, on her forearms like a promise, her eyebrows confirming, her upper lip waxed.

Her eyes were so dark that I could not return the stare, and her nostrils flared, while her lips could have modeled for a cosmetic surgeon. My sense of honor and dignity did not allow me to look below her neck. I hated the lecherous man and did not want her to think me so. Even then I felt vaguely guilty at these thoughts. I had imagined that I would never look at another woman in this way — especially not now that Nicki had returned into my life.

"Yes, come in, Ansinoé." I elected to be standard but feared it had not worked, as my feet slid on the carpet. She passed beneath my armpit as I closed the door, and swayed slightly in the middle of the hallway. I caught the passing glimpse I'd denied earlier and noticed her heavily disguised rounded figure. She wore what looked like a doctor's coat — white with tartan collar, a raincoat maybe, Burberry. I caught myself imagining that perhaps she wore nothing beneath it, but discarded this quickly. Why were my feelings about this girl already beginning to run away with themselves? Her long legs made her look African. I turned my head, slightly appalled at my voyeurism and need, not wishing to embarrass myself, or her, and not wanting Nicki to detect what was happening inside me, if she was watching this event.

"Sit?" I offered.

"Thanks." We sat in the main living room, the room with the vaulted redwood, church-like ceiling, the room with the antique tables Nicki had bought in London, the George Smith sofas likewise, the carpet, the chairs, the huge fireplace mantle, the African table, the everything Nicki.

Ansinoé sat and crossed her long legs and twisted them in that impossible way models do when they sit down.

"So, can I get you something to drink? Tea, coffee, vodka?" She smiled slightly and declined, but relaxed a touch.

"This is a difficult mission," she said, her head down, her long, thick black hair over her eyes for a moment.

"Mission? Are you religious?" I suddenly wondered whom I had invited into my house, though to be honest it didn't much intimidate me anyway, she didn't look freakish.

"I know, sounds a bit culty, doesn't it?" She hesitated and sighed again. "I'm not from a cult, and I'm not particularly religious, really, though I was brought up as a Quaker in a devout family." She hesitated again. "Why am I telling you this?"

"Don't know, but I'm okay with it. Talk about whatever you want, though I might give you a bill on the way out." I smiled, trying to calm her.

"Sorry. You're so sweet. I'm here because I've been researching you."

"My God. Plucky, aren't you?"

"I guess so, though I'm banking on you going for naïve, innocent, you know, spy-girl."

"How can a spy be innocent?"

"Right, well, not really a spy. More of a research student interested in phenomena. I don't want to hurt you, or cheat you, or anything. That's why I'm here."

"What did you find?"

"I'm not sure. I'm really not sure. Just something that I want to be involved in."

They sat together, already so close. I could feel the chemistry between them, and wondered how intense my jealousy would become if this continued into more intimate realms. I knew that I could only do what I had been doing so far, allowing the space for Gideon to see her (did I have such power?), giving him space to play with her, tease her, discover who she was, and maybe get some pleasure and help from her. I could not feel her as well as I could feel him, but as they began to connect I experienced her better, as though through him and his growing feelings for her my power to heal expanded. Occasionally it seemed as though I was seeing the future — knowing the inevitability of events that would transpire, but this was probably only my knowledge of Gideon and his passion for dark, hirsute, young, pretty women. His early passion for me had been because of the way I looked, the hair, the darkness, the fullness of my body. Now here was another, but unlike me she was alive with a heart beating in her chest, as I had been. How jealous would I become? How could I prevent this? I could only watch like a sick ghost, and try to be wise — though in this I was not.

"Did you see only me in your research, or someone else too?" he asked.

"No, not just you, at least I don't think so."

"Did you get a picture?"

"Yes. Well I er *took* a picture of you."

"Really?" He smiled and moved closer still. "Show me."

Ansinoé opened her bag and pulled out the envelope containing the print, opened it, and set it on the African table, close to her African legs.

Gideon leaned forward too, and their heads came close enough for him to feel the static in her hair. They looked for a long time. He felt the hair on the back of his neck stand up, and tears came into his eyes. It was me, though the photo looked like something out of a ghost movie. There was no real shape to the pictured background behind Gideon in the library, and yet there was something distinctly me (why was I staying away he wondered? Or perhaps I was watching all this.)

He sat back into the generous sofa and held the photograph, his breath coming a little short. This picture was of his wife, his lover of so many years, a lover so strong and caring, so bonded with him that she would return even after death. As he looked at it, it felt like a kind of spiritual wedding photo, and the thought made him smile.

He caught his breath and closed his eyes for a moment. He wanted to talk but couldn't.

Ansinoé sat quietly, making the space for him to recover, looking slightly embarrassed.

"Why are you doing this?" Gideon asked.

"Because I'm worried about you, and because I'm fascinated by what's apparently happening to you — by phenomena like this. There's quite a bit of talk on campus, and this photograph makes it all very real."

"And it gives you license to investigate me?" He didn't really mean it, as he'd already become quite fond of her.

"I guess not, except that it has more to do with a sense of, I don't know, concern, really. I have no interest in selling you to the public, quite the opposite in fact. And anyway, can't you see how fascinating this is, a genuine ghost picture?"

"Why would I need your help? And as you say, if this is a genuine ghost picture, why would you not want to sell it to the *National Enquirer.* They'd love it."

"I don't want to do that. I hate those people and that stuff. They would think it a fake anyway, and I don't need the money. I ... I'm just fascinated, and excited, that's all."

"Okay, okay. I'm sorry to doubt you, but we never met before, and this is a very sensitive issue for me. I had no idea anyone was out there taking pictures of us. I never even imagined that a camera would pick up the image at all. It's incredible."

"It is, and it seems to me that the spirit world is maybe not what it seems sometimes." She stopped in mid-sentence.

"And?" He leaned forward and turned toward her. She remained silent, as though trying to form precise words.

"People see things. They see visions of holy individuals. Mary, for example, probably one of the most common visions of all. People believe that because a vision of Mary has appeared before them, that somehow that's hugely significant."

"I don't follow. What do you mean?"

"Perhaps Mary may not always be the benevolent, compassionate, beautiful spirit we imagine she should be. Maybe even Mary is not just a saintly spirit, but a real, even playful spirit."

"You mean, these mischievous Marys are not always Mary-like at all?" The idea of a good spirit being actually like any normal personality was something Gideon hadn't considered. And the chemistry between them grew as they talked. It was written all over their faces. What did this make me feel? I was a spirit after all — why should I feel jealousy — still suffer the troubles of the body and mind? Was I still somehow alive?

"Well, kind of, yes. Why not? Why do we assume that Mary is always only going to be saintly?"

"It's rather a neat idea actually. Did you dream all this up yourself?" The professor spoke.

"We're very naïve about the spirit world. We expect the disembodied to be honest, or at least obvious. We think that somehow when the living pass over, even if they were one thing during their lives, somehow when they die they become obvious — good, believable, bad, without integrity — whatever. You know, everything is black and white, no character deviations and complexities."

"Well, you may look innocent, but you sure as hell aren't. I'm supposed to be the professor and you've got better ideas than I do." We both knew that he complimented her as part of his seduction. His eyes roamed her face and then her neck, and down and down — my Gideon, being furtive! "So what does that make humans? Stupid?"

"Well, naïve, as I said. We project onto the spirit world what we believe it should be in our dreams. We see what we want to see, and we hear what we want to hear. The spirit world is often only too happy to give us exactly what we want."

"So you mean I might be seeing the Nicki I want to see, just to make me feel better about losing her."

"Maybe. I don't know. It's not always like that, because if the spirit was a truly attached and loving partner, rather than some remote archetype, the

119

relationship may have some independence of the projection we put upon it."

"You mean, she really loves me still." Yes.

"Yes. And it seems to me that the photograph shows that there is an independent entity there, rather than an entity fashioned by your mind. Mind you, this is all theory. I could be completely wrong."

"All sounds quite convincing, actually. Are you doing a paper on this?"

"I've made a life of it. I've been doing this work since I was ten years old. My father and mother too."

"Are they dead?"

"Yes."

"Do you see them?"

"All the time."

They were silent.

So there it was, she was a kindred spirit! He had found someone who knew the story, who spoke the language, and she was covered in flesh! This was the first time I felt uncomfortable about my lifetime partner. I could not be the voyeur now. It was finally time for some degree of separation, and yet I could not remove myself from the scene. It suddenly became evident that I did not control my own movements, my own destination. Then came the questions — where am I, and who am I? What was I really doing here? Was there anywhere else for me to go? And then I changed to self-chiding — maybe this was just a drama in my own mind. Why should making love to another living, fleshly woman mean he didn't love me anymore? And this gave me several answers to my questions. I was here and could not go anywhere else because I still loved him, and with that love came all the opportunities for questions, for love was not only love, but possessiveness, fear, and therefore jealousy, and doubt, which produced immobility and loss of self. I had lost my flesh and yet retained it. I was still in my body even though outside it. With this series of realizations came an instant transformation. Suddenly, in a flash of light, I found myself no longer blinded by the humanity of my previous condition. I saw for the first time that after death we hold onto life because we remain alive. Death does not kill, it only changes.

# SEVEN

I didn't intend to make love with Ansinoé. I don't think she intended to make love with me, but our intentions were not fulfilled. It was an event, though it began clumsily enough. I hadn't any idea of how much stored tension there was in my body, and certainly I had no idea of the extent of energy in hers. We literally attacked each other.

"Do you think they're watching now?" I asked her as she ripped off my shirt.

"My parents are dead." She fumbled.

"But you said they..." A button from my shirt pinged against the window.

"They were Quakers. Quakers don't want to know about this sort of thing. What about Nicki?" She rolled up her blouse like a schoolgirl trying to be neat.

"She's generally tactful, but this is the first time for me."

"Good, let's make it good. I didn't know how much ...how much I needed you."

We went upstairs and fell onto the bed, tackling one another like football players, pulling and pushing, levering and bouncing. It wasn't so much a passionate encounter as an encounter with passion. We didn't expect it to rush at us like a raging bull. Everything was on automatic. We went so far into the deep end that words were swallowed before they reached the outside air. I can't tell you what she said, and I can't remember anything that I said — even if it made any sense at all, for it was all swallowing, and absorption, bruises for which we had not felt the blows, kisses of which we remembered no flavor, and genitals that collided. It was not simply an act of sex but a play with love, for it carried love's combined uncertainties as we explored and disturbed. We did not hinder one another's progress at this early point in our intimacy, but there were hints that we might if we were to do it again.

Eventually, silence spread across our bodies. We did not envelope one another, we did not process, we did not admit or feel guilt. We simply stopped and rested like two animals.

Naked, she was more beautiful than clothed. I surveyed her body while she lay there with her eyes closed. She was long on the bed, her hair luxurious on the sheets, her shape fuller than I had imagined. The skin was brown, and her eyelashes long and black, the eyebrows thick and black, the body hair astonishingly bushy, under her arms, beneath her belly.

But I couldn't sleep. There was too much to consider in all this. This encounter might stop Nicki from coming again. Did this mean that I had to acknowledge her departure? Was this the vehicle by which all the excitement of my continued love affair with a ghost would end? Did I love this woman? I looked at her again and all I could see was the deep, black, ranging hair across her belly and down her legs. I loved that, for sure, but she wasn't only her hair.

"What shall we do?" she said suddenly. "Will Nicki mind?"

"I was wondering, I guess I'll find out soon enough. She's not here now, maybe she won't find out."

"You're kidding. You mean when she's not here she doesn't know what you're up to?"

"That's a thought." I took up what remained of my shirt, and headed for the bathroom, recovering my pants and socks along the way. Ansinoé remained on the crumpled sheets.

Ansinoé left after we had spoken a little more about the earthquake, the nature of my physical condition, my life with Nicki. She refused lunch and went her way promising a return soon. I thought I didn't want her to. I sat alone until Tashy came visiting. I fed him the turkey and ground beef that someone had left at the front entrance during the night. Was it dear Jennifer?

I couldn't eat. I had no appetite at all, and the sexual encounter with Ansinoé had left me entirely sated, but somehow troubled, like an unwilling adulterer. I sat at my computer and worried slightly over not going into work. But the idea just left me cold. Maybe I'd try to attend a lecture or two.

Where was she? Where was my Nicki?

That night I flew in my dreams. I was walking with a bunch of friends. They were friends, but I could not identify them. I did not know who they were. Suddenly, without warning I lifted off and spread my arms and flew through the air way up high above them. As I came down to earth again and landed smoothly on the ground like a heron, Nicki stood beside me.

"Have you missed me?"

"Yes. Where've you been?"

"Do you still have the kiss?"

I nodded.

"Shall we walk between the trees together?"

I nodded again and we set off along the forest edge of my dream, watching the pelicans dive into the Pacific. It was summer and very early morning, and there was no one about. The air smelled of ocean and the sky never had a cloud in its whole history. We walked and walked and spoke not a single word, then sat down on a piece of driftwood on the beach. She was quite real beside me, so real I could touch her and smell her. This was the nicest way to meet with her because all my senses were intact, and she was physical, as though we were living together again. She felt closer and more attentive, as though she knew about my lovemaking with Ansinoé and suffered from insecurity and jealousy, just as she would have done in life. I wanted to reassure her, but doing so seemed vulgar and obvious. Mostly I didn't want her now to think that the lovemaking could damage what we had between us for so many years. I guess she knew all that without me having to open my mouth and make excuses. She nuzzled her head on my shoulder and tucked her arm beneath mine, and we sat there together forever. Then we walked again.

"What about this extension of my life, Nicki? Is this a gift from you?"

"Yes, I suppose, though I have no real idea how it happened — part of your vitality perhaps, a result of the kiss, that magical kiss."

"It means we won't be together on your side of the veil for longer."

"Oh, don't think of the future. Think only of how much you will enjoy the present — a present from me of more present." She giggled. We walked in silence for a moment.

"I'd like to show you something of my world." She stopped close to the lapping waves and took my hands in hers.

"Yes, you said you might." My heart began to beat faster.

She let go of my hands and turned around, backing gently into my arms and leaning her head against my shoulder, like Tashy rubbing. A few yards away from us a tree stood, about fifteen feet tall, very young, with

126

large, voluptuous rich green leaves. The leaves were like those of the money trees I had seen in California, thick, muscular, and abundant, which I guessed was why it had that name. But this tree had leaves five times bigger than the money tree, though just as thick, and they drooped from their own weight.

"This tree began to grow here after you stopped the earthquake. It grows only in my world, here beyond the veil, and it helps to feed us." She leaned back her face to look up at me, questioning whether I understood.

"I didn't imagine that spirits ate anything." I didn't understand, of course, but then nothing Nicki ever said to me was entirely clear to my addled and primitive brain.

"You know the story of the time traveler and the butterfly?"

"No."

"A time traveler went in a time machine into the distant past. When he stepped out of the time machine, his clumsy foot crushed a butterfly on the ground, and in that instant he vanished and was no more, in fact had never been." She looked back at the tree before us. "This tree is born because you stepped on the butterfly. Clumsy!"

I woke, or so I thought, troubled and sweating again, mostly I guessed from the booze I'd drunk after

Ansinoé had left the prior night. Nevertheless, there was also something very weird going on. I put it down to the dream, being significant in my memory. Was this how Nicki would visit me in the future? What happened to the journey she had promised me into her world? Tashy was spread out full length on the sheepskin rug beside Nicki's side of the bed. Perhaps it had been him nuzzling my head and not Nicki. But what about the tree she showed me?

I pulled up the blinds on the windows and noticed something different about the garden, though I couldn't really say what it was. Everything seemed greener somehow, more beautiful, with more flowers, somehow richer in quality. I showered, ate, and went outside, still wondering about what Nicki had shown me on the beach by the forest in the dream. "Clumsy," she called me, for "stepping on a butterfly," she said, another of her weird riddles.

I began the day insignificantly. I went to Whole Foods and spent too much money on food, wondering all the time why I should bother — did a long-life being need to eat so much? Ansinoé hadn't told me about such things, and neither had Dr. Bauer. I felt hungry, though, and seemed to be losing weight. Also a full refrigerator felt like a good idea, with all this insecurity around. It took me an hour to fill my cart. It seemed right somehow.

Pulling Nicki's car, filled with grocery goodies, into the entrance I saw the greenness of the garden once more, and went over to take a closer look. All around the edges of the huge tree that blossomed each spring with pink flowers were tiny growing sprouts that had not been there before, so far as I could recollect. They covered the entire area of the earth and resembled small trees, as they had thick stems, thicker than plants. On the new branches of these small trees were tiny, bulbous green leaves like the money plants that grew elsewhere on my front patio. There were so many of them I wondered how on earth they could have grown so rapidly.

I remained sitting on the wooden ledge that separated the garden from the front yard and realized that I never did that. I never sat still in my life, always on the move, doing, making, worrying, dying. Just to be still was so good. Everything around me echoed my stillness and silence. The birds stopped singing, and the wind stopped blowing.

It was as though I was suddenly in heaven here, surrounded by this strange new sense of the beauty of nature, and what looked like some of the same trees Nicki had shown me in the dream were growing here and there — small shoots sprouting up. And then it came to me that I was still in the same dream, still not awakened from the walk with Nicki on the beach amidst the trees. Was this some kind of lucid continuation in sleep — or what?

There was a merging between the reality that I was familiar with and the rest of what was happening to me. It felt as though Nicki was introducing me to her reality, and that prior to arrival there I was being carried through a barrier; a semi-dream, semi-real world which formed like a no-man's-land. Perhaps this was the veil itself. Yet they had no name, these trees. Their identity was missing and somehow that seemed appropriate.

There was a sensation, as I sat in the garden, that I was traveling. It felt like my body was accelerating into a different dimension, a little like I imagine a pilot feels inside a spacecraft at high velocity. Yet I was also still sitting silently there, surrounded by flowers. I had started here from a state of absolute silence in my transforming garden of fresh colors and beauty, and as I moved through the dream, everything became entirely appropriate, as though the track were laid down as I stepped forward.

From that moment on I had the sense of being in heaven, though not quite as the Christians would have it. It was not paved with gold, and its corridors were not lined with the elaborate foliage and soft messages of perfect peace and goodwill, though a god may be in residence there. Heaven is as unbelievable as time itself, and as believable as this moment. All this flashed through my mind on an unfamiliar level.

My surroundings changed now, from the bright sunny garden about my house to a kind of rooted darkness, deeply heavy and daunting, with shadows that echoed still deeper, as though the devil himself might have ventured here. I swear there were a million souls in this place, roaming amongst endless corridors, passing through innumerable doors, and casting their emptiness over billions of dull, grimy puddles of water that had dripped from as many roofs of Gormenghast.

Here was evidence of ancient rituals, "footprints ankle-deep in stone." And here was I. Did Nicki really take me here? Was this her realm at last, a tour of the spirit world for me? Or was this the work of some other mischievous spirit?

And where was Nicki? I tried to make sense out of it all and felt deeply disoriented and frightened. But I had stopped moving, and stood at the edge of something I could not yet see clearly.

I hesitated there at the edge of this unclear "place." My mind had already suspended disbelief, for the picture was so unlikely, so dramatic. And yet something knew where I was, for I had the distinct sense of guidance in it all. Something knew all about this, and smiled gently at me, as I worried and gasped.

I was at the edge of a movie that was about to begin in someone else's life, and there was an entrance to it that I had not realized was there before now. I knew that I could have walked back through the door and shut it, and that when I opened it again, the same scene might not be there at all. I knew also that I could step across the threshold and enter the dream, the reality, the whatever-the-hell-it-was that stood before me. And I knew that if I didn't enter, I'd have a lot of explaining to do to some being, some wizard that inhabited only my own imagination. Perhaps this was my unconscious — a deep realm of my own being reflected across time and space.

And so I stepped forward, and at the very second my body moved beyond the doorway, the picture transformed completely and I stood at the cross-road of a beautiful, bright, summer day. Long fronds fell from the banyan trees around me, like the vines in a tropical jungle. Hundreds of bicycles were parked by the side of the road, and a woman dressed in brightly colored clothes burned a bonfire close by, warming her hands.

I stood transfixed, unable to orient myself or be sure at all that I wasn't in a completely new dream. The thought crossed my mind from that same silent witness, that of course I *was* in a dream, a dream created by my wife's spirit. She had carried me into the transforming spirit world of her own making.

Here I was truly lost.

I had traveled from darkness into light. There had been uncertainty, doubt, even fear, whereas here was light, beauty, and anticipation — the other side of some invisible coin. I felt a certain rejoicing in my heart, that I would encounter something unimaginably breathtaking here.

Which way to turn? I closed my eyes and opened them again just to make absolutely sure that this was the place I could expect to remain in. Nothing changed. I turned left.

A few yards ahead of me walked a man and woman. As I drew closer to them I began to notice the houses beside the road. To my left was a most astonishing palace, with white entrance portals and pillars, massive porticoes and beautiful ornate gardens. I stopped and gaped at it. Here stood massive wealth and status, and next to this giant building there was another of the same — an extraordinary piece of architecture that must have arisen out of considerable profit. The young couple entered the huge house and were met by others, all beautifully dressed and happily mixing with what looked like Gypsy girls carrying gorgeous children.

Next door were lesser dwellings, and as I drew level, there was one that particularly attracted me — a small hut, maybe big enough for one room, which stood a few yards set back from the road. It was a mere box, a single room encased in plaster, a light on the front, a bolt on the door, a step up to the entrance. I turned toward it. I knew that it contained something for me.

The front yard was blocked by a huge pile of sand and gravel. Building work seemed imminent. There was a small child bent upon the ground nearby, murmuring stories to her friend, who sat beside her on the grass. I realized then that this was dusk.

Stepping up to the front of the small dwelling, I hesitated. There was clearly someone inside, though I knew nothing of whom or why. What should I say? Why was I here?

I knocked on the white door and briefly, amid my doubtful thoughts, I looked about me, as one does at front doors. The bird sounds were exquisitely beautiful, and I watched a huge black crow sitting above my head on a branch of a strangely shaped tree. Was this the same crow I had met in California? The gardens around the tiny hut were carefully tended, and there was a small bonfire burning near the center and an old woman squatted down. Two children tottered into my dream to see what I was all about. They were so small and so perfectly made, with a bright beauty, their eyes deep-deep brown and shining bright.

There was an aura of silence everywhere, even amid the sounds of distant truck horns and train whistles and the cawing birds of so many varieties. The very air about me stood completely still, with such perfect wonder, such absolute meditation, that I could have remained in that spot forever.

The door opened. Of course, had I thought for even a moment, I would have known who would be there standing in expectation. Nicki pulled back the door wide, stepped out immediately, and wrapped both her arms about me, literally dragging me into the room. Her face was beaming with excitement, shining with joy and pleasure, and she spent no moments waiting to put her soft full lips against mine and kiss me, though the kiss was short and somehow more delicate than her hug had promised. It was as though she made something of a performance of her enthusiasm

134

and then checked herself. But she was truly there in all her glorious beauty this time. Her body so soft and so solid, her breasts so full, so astonishingly full and so pressing. The very act of grasping her in my arms was an act of worship, bringing me soundly into the present without a single thought in my head. With Nicki I was entirely alone in all subjective judgments. No one else could corroborate the content of my vision; no one could comment on her character, criticize her virtues into vandalism to compensate the tincture of rose petals that floated constantly before my eyes. I knew then that I, Gideon's ghost, was Nicki's lover, and that I was still absolutely this woman's slave. No other lover could ever replace her, even though she might one day depart from me.

Her face turned to shyness, her body slipping into that eminent posture that women adopt when they seduce — the toe turned in, the hip gently forward, the shoulder too, the face turned down, the lip-touching finger, a genetic posture inherited from a thousand generations.

She slipped past me and closed the door behind us. I watched her transfixed. She was human and completely herself, and here with me. No designs or camouflage.

"Well, Mr. Gideon, what do you think you are doing here?"

"If I knew that." I sat on the bed and bounced up and down. She laughed and guided me to the cane seat, gently pushing me down to rest.

135

I sat, and for a moment there was nothing to say or do. The birds indicated their lack of interest, and the smell of the bonfire outside drifted across my nose. Nicki was still ghostly, though she was more real than ever she had been since she died. She stood before me for a moment as though examining some trophy, her head turned to one side slightly, her hands interlinked below her belly, the thumbs vaguely caressing one another like lovers taken for granted.

Her face was virtually expressionless, though one eyebrow was slightly higher than the other. Her eyes sparkled now even more than they had when her shadow was stronger than her body. Her nostrils were slightly flared, and she twitched her nose at that instant as though listening to my thoughtful commentary.

"So? Where are we? What is this?" I asked.

"I suppose you could call it my world, but it's yours, too."

"How intriguing! And how exactly did you bring me here, underneath the house, over the hills and far away?"

"I didn't bring you here and it's not anywhere near the house, except that it's next door." There was again that reassuring tone of the long-loved wife.

She moved again to a step away from me, slightly uncomfortable with my presence. I was disconcerted and then reassured with every movement she made. I did not know her at all, and yet I knew her totally. I could not read even her most obvious movements, and yet they were entirely familiar. Only now, way into my own future telling this tale, do I know that at this resurgence of our complete physical awareness of one another she was at last a little afraid of me, touched by me in a place that disconcerted her, trapping her into feeling she might identify once more and therefore have to love me again in the ways that she did when she was in her body. Was this all a performance brought about by my unfaithfulness with Ansinoé? Was this a supreme effort undertaken by a ghost to bring back intense human, passionate feelings? Was I wrong on all counts?

A silence in the tiny cramped room made us both stop. Our glances always came back to one another, the light dimming slightly as the day came to an end, the sounds of the birds still present. We fell then and there in love again, but only God knew of it.

She took my hand and laced her slim fingers into mine, leading me out of the room.

I felt that I walked at the center of an enigma. I could not fit anything around me into what had been my life before, but I felt willing to wait for developments, trusting my fate into my lover's arms.

The early dusk had fallen upon this magic presence, and the light had given up its dance.

"This is just for fun," she whispered in my ear. "And to show you how clumsy you have been, look."

I watched to where her finger pointed and immediately saw the same trees that she had shown me on the dream beach in California. Only here they grew in such richness and abundance as though they occupied the whole area of land on one side of the road. The flowers and vegetation were also as rich and colorful as around the house, and people were picking the leaves off the branches and filling baskets to overflowing.

"This is what happens when you step on the butterfly. This place is a dream of somewhere that could exist in your world, and it can all happen because of our presence in it and the love we share forever!"

We walked through a maze of pathways leading in all directions, the borders ranged with hosts of those exotic, leafy trees and flowers that leaned over the pathway and stroked us as we past. There were couples walking arm-in-arm before us and toward us, smiling and laughing.

My apprehension deepened until we arrived at a huge, tent-roofed gathering place from which emerged music that would remain with me for the rest of my life. As we walked about the edge of this enormous space, the floor made entirely of marble, I noticed thirty or forty people moving inside. Movement is barely the word — they were whirling in a manner that I can see now in my mind's eye — wide flowing skirts riding on a deep ripple several feet beyond their circling bodies. Their heads were tilted sideways and the colors of their clothing a bright blue in uniformity with the dance. The music had a powerful repetitive rhythm that immediately captured both my heart and my body. Those who danced moved with such perfect symmetry that everyone including me became transfixed. I sat down on the marble floor, almost falling over, letting myself go into a gentle trance.

"I want to dance like that. How can I do that?" I asked at last.

"Soon. You will do everything soon." Nicki tugged at my arm. "Come, I must show you something else first."

We moved away from the marble-floored hall and the dancers and came to a larger building in the shape of a pyramid. Here there were many people milling about, sitting on walls in the glorious sunlight, chatting, hugging, reading, or sitting totally still and in silence. People ambled in and out of the building, which seemed to be a major hubbub of activity inside.

It was such a contrast to the whirling beauty of the dancers that I felt a sense of confusion. Everyone was deeply concentrated on what they were doing, but there was also all this joy. People smiled a lot, kissed each other, one would gently stroke the face of another, while two others would stand in a long hug together. There was the singsong of laughter, giggling, and bright, happy talk.

"What on earth is this place?" I asked.

"This is the gathering place."

"Gathering for what?"

"Well, just gathering, for fun." She waved her hand in a broad gesture, as if this were answer enough.

"I don't understand — no purpose?" I turned to look at her, puzzled now, my uncertainty rising out of human suspicion.

"Purpose?" She stared at me for a moment, looked vaguely up at the ceiling and back at me again. "The purpose of fun. You know, like people do, occupying themselves, resting, whatever."

"Occupying themselves, resting from what?"

She frowned at me as though I must be stupid. "You know, work and play and all that. No one needs to work, Gideon. Everything is provided peacefully and without anxiety. They all have what they need, food, activity, love, lots of love, and play."

I stared at her, my brain ticking almost aloud. She smiled with the pride and delight of one who helped create what lay before us. I continued to look at her with absolute blank astonishment.

"And you will come here one day," she said suddenly, as though it were obvious.

"I will?"

"Yes, everyone comes here on their quest, one day."

"What quest?"

"That's for you to find out, just as I am. And as you find out you'll discover that the pathway of the quest goes on forever, and as it progresses it gets narrower and narrower until eventually you have no choice but to follow it. No one else will see your pathway, nor will you see theirs, though everyone has one, few know even of their own." She looked at me for a moment, and then back at the surrounding activity, smiling once more at this place as though I was no longer there.

For me it was all a little too much, and I began to feel the back of my neck growing prickly and hot, together with a certain weakness at the knees. A deep sense of insecurity was also arising in my heart, for here I stood in the midst of a dream with no escape, no known exit route. I was in the land of the dead, after all, and the attendant uncertainties and that pervasive darkness hovered about me. This was the deep, ancient magic that she had often hinted at and which now I experienced also.

And yet as I stood there in this strange place I began to sense another presence, a holy presence within and without. In the background, the music had changed, and I could hear lilting flutes and soft accompaniment, sounds that lifted my spirit away from the mind's chatter, giving me a new space of mystery, accepted rather than feared.

Nicki led me away from the pyramid and out again into the open where the light had dropped completely now. My uncertainty began to change into a kind of happy trance, a state in which all responsibilities and stresses were taken from me, leaving me with a sense of total emptiness. I smelled the air, clean and soft with flower essences and a special flavor that I had never experienced before. It was the smell of freedom.

In that moment, I began to make some sense of it all, coming as it did in a flash of realization. Everything that happened to me was coinciding with my needs in that moment. As I felt happy, so the mind came in to bring doubt, and as the doubt affected my heart, so I felt sad and lost. As I questioned this, the answers flowed in this dream reality and brought back reward and a sense of love and freedom. I was making it all happen, not Nicki. She was my guide and mentor, but my own heart was leading the way and granting my prayers every moment, instantly.

We sat close by in a temple area with Buddha statues and a carefully sculptured garden.

"So, shall I tell you a little about this place? You look more receptive than when you arrived."

"Yes," I said.

"In a way this is a future, but it's also my world, the world where human frailty and foolishness have given way to mutual love and concern. This is a dream for you to enjoy, a world for you to dream of. Somewhere you and I can visit together whenever we want to give you comfort from my departure from the body. You will help me to fashion it. Then there will be your world of human, living people, and my world of dreams and beauty and we'll make it happen together."

"Can anyone come here?" I asked.

"Yes, of course. In fact everyone does. Everyone who knows the dead, the spirit world, comes here, though it will be different for each individual on each path that he or she takes. This is the gathering place of souls, Gideon, after life, and before life, this is where we all come together and rest." I looked about one more time, and remembered my most important thought, running to Nicki once more.

"So you'll always be with me?" I looked at her, feeling distinctly the victim of my own weakness.

"Of course. I will always be with you, in all your everlasting life, Gideon. Let go of fear. You don't need it anymore."

# EIGHT

He sat in the garden outside our home again, surrounded by the burgeoning trees and flowers, looking rather stunned, no doubt wondering what had happened to him and whether he was now finally out of the dream. There was a sort of light in his eyes as he began to comprehend what had been a mystery before. Ansinoé sat beside him now, her Range Rover parked nearby in the driveway. I had repaired my doubts and fears, repaired my jealousies by taking him somewhere she could never take him, by offering him my world instead of hers, and a vague notion of guilt twisted its way into my heart. When would I be free of these ridiculous notions that preoccupied the so-called living each minute of each day, and evidently the non-living also?

Dr. Bauer and Jennifer were on the scene with her with Gideon's test results. These three women would bring him down to earth and help relieve his uncertainties. One of them was holding a tulip from the garden. The flowers had evidently grown larger rather more quickly than they should have done. Where was normal reality for him now? He felt it had taken a back seat during these times of crumpled dreams. He wondered for a moment if the dream was still happening?

Dr. Bauer greeted him with warmth, her huge brown eyes smiling at him out of her ruffled hair.

"Is the garden more beautiful or am I in a dream?" Ansinoé said, holding the stem of a tulip. Jennifer looked glum and irritated with her, no doubt sensing the reason for her friendliness.

"Yes, in my dream." Gideon answered, and I heard his mind jump and his heart beat faster. How could everything have become so much brighter and more colorful and beautiful? What miracle had I created now, he thought.

"Did you plant all this color yourself?" Ansinoé came toward him.

"Why should you think that?" Gideon began gathering up the grocery bags and the women each took a bag and trudged up the stairs behind him and before him. Jennifer lunged forward taking one of his bags and refusing to give it back, carrying two bags into the house. Gideon's mind was spinning. What would he tell them? What was true and what was false? I couldn't help smiling to myself as I watched him struggle with it all. I had spannered his works again — thrown a googly, as the British cricketer would love to say.

I watched them all from the bedroom window, interacting in ways that they could hardly know the significance of. It seemed to me that I had become enlightened, that my being was suffused with light, and that everything I saw now was lit with the flash of that enlightenment. Gideon was still delighted at the change in his garden, and with the journey I had taken him on through the realms of resting souls.

He had not been able to separate dream from reality, still believing, as all humans do, that there is something different between the two. There had been the dream of the "magic" trees, and then the reality/dream of my world, and now came the real version of that dream, in the eyes of the woman he had so recently made love to. He didn't yet see that Ansinoé had adopted his nature in the moment that they joined one another. So caught up was he, as I had been, in fear, doubt, retreat, that the reality of their joining escaped him, though I saw that it had not escaped Ansinoé.

Here was the fruit of their bodies, and the fruit of my kiss on his forehead, born and bred by Mother Earth, consummated by our continued love. Nature had somehow responded to our relationship across the veil, with the birth of beauty from my kiss. This brought me joy, though I watched with humor as his supporters and friends unfolded Gideon's comprehension.

I was grateful for these three women in my life, and for the fact that they had arrived just at the moment they had. Their grounded and loving natures, each in their turn, brought me soundly back to earth again after Nicki's departure — if departed she had. I always had the sense that she hovered somewhere in the background, and I vaguely wondered how she engineered her appearances and disappearances.

"So, what have you been up to Gideon? A bit of gardening? Seems like it's everywhere." Dr. Bauer set down her bag of groceries, very un-doctor-like now.

"What's everywhere?" Ansinoé asked, returning to the conversation after she delivered a large carton of milk to the freezer.

"Not in the freezer." Jennifer snatched the milk from Ansinoé's hands.

"I don't know — all these wonderful plants and flowers and trees. Or has it always been like this? Another of Gideon's secrets."

"What secrets?" Jennifer muttered, a flush radiating.

"Can I tell them?" Dr. Bauer turned to me.

"Sure. Why not? We're all friends here," I said. "Frankly, after the last few weeks nothing would surprise me anyway."

"Your friend here has an extended life expectancy." Dr. Bauer smiled slightly as if to reduce the phenomenon into something purely medical.

"Extended? How do you know this?" Jennifer turned to Dr. Bauer.

"He's developed, somehow, we don't know how, some sort of youthful condition. He'll probably live to be a hundred or more, unless a bus knocks him down."

"How wonderful." Ansinoé patted me on the shoulder, and Jennifer frowned again.

"I think it's Nicki," she said.

"Who's Nicki?" Dr. Bauer sat next to me as I peeled an orange.

"My wife, she's dead." I said blandly.

"Oh, yes, of course. That was quite recent, yes?"

"A month or so ago, I guess. I've almost forgotten when, actually."

"Oh." Dr Bauer seemed unsure how to respond to this last statement. Ansinoé and Jennifer smiled, in unison for the first time.

"It's okay. I'm figuring it all out, that's all. Tell us more about this new physical condition of mine."

"Well. You're definitely aging more slowly than normal. It's not unique, though very rare. When you're eighty you'll still look like a fifty year old and maybe at around a hundred you'll begin to look and feel like an old man. We don't really know much about it except that it happens in certain mountain areas of Russia more than anywhere else, though not quite so suddenly as in your case. They're an ethnic group who have hereditary qualities of slow aging. They regularly have elders aged over 150, though mostly people don't believe them!" She smiled.

"And this condition developed recently in him?" Ansinoé asked, gazing at me rather more fondly than she should.

"So far as we can tell, in the past few weeks."

They cooked together and set the food out on the main dining table, the first time the table had been used since Gideon had given up his cooking frenzy after I left the body. They set out the best cutlery and glassware and everything was beautiful and candlelit. They all got drunk on expensive champagne, talking and celebrating their lives and the miracle of Gideon's new love affair with life.

And that night I dreamed again of the world that Nicki had taken me to, and we talked about the so-called reality of our lives together. Now I began to realize that "reality" was a misnomer. I was as much in reality here in my dreams with Nicki as anywhere else.

"Is this your doing — the beautiful garden, my extended life? Did you make all this for me?"

"Yes."

"What's going to happen — where's all this leading?"

"I don't have an inside track — I'm watching just like you. There's no Big Brother or God or saints.

149

There's nothing more than is right here now. All the thoughts, the ideas, all the gurus, all the ancient spirits are inconsequential in the face of the ultimate truth that you and I have shared."

We were silent for a moment, and then I dared to ask her to be my oracle.

"Tell me why humans are so misguided?"

"You want a lecture about humans? I'm barely past human myself." She smiled. We sat by the entrance to her small room in the dream world, and I leaned into her slightly.

"Humanity has a particular purpose which has been imposed by itself, not from the outside, but from within itself — within all of you as a group. You believe, through the presence of the mind and of religion, that each individual human is separate from all others and therefore from God, that there is somehow a gap between the skin of one person and the skin of another, and that each skin is also separate from the rest of the universe. This separation provides all the necessary requirements for suffering, anxiety, fear, doubt, lack of love, etc.

"If you were to alter that self-perception and replace it with another, one that I see to be a correct one, your condition in life would alter completely. This new self-perception would be one that says you are not separate at all. It would illustrate to you that in fact the molecules and atoms of the air and the flowing energy between your skins, and between you and the spirit world also — between you and God — enter your bodies and mix and match inside your bodies. It would show also that all the thoughts and emotions, and circumstances of life are part of that connectivity, and that there is no gap between you but a continuous flowing of energy and substance that makes you entirely connected. You are essentially one being, one mind, and one existence all the way to God.

"All the energies and atoms of both the so-called living world and the spirit world are as much one with all as the grains of sand on a beach or the stars in the sky. In this way you are made of the universe — you *are* the universe and the universe *is* you. This is why some people can make contact with others and with the dead, because we're all living and dead together at the same time.

"If you are separate then you are essentially unconscious, because how can you be conscious if you have separated yourself from life? All you have then is a split mind — your mind examining your mind.

"Connectivity, oneness, is everything, and it provides all manner of wonderful answers once you find it. All important questions are answered immediately when you realize that everything you do in life is connected to everything else you do."

I gazed at her in wonder. "When did you experience all this?"

"It started shortly after I left my body and continues to develop, though I haven't really got it totally right yet! Without a body there is the potential of pure consciousness, and with pure consciousness there is pure awareness, though I am still not in that pure state yet, because I am so attached still to your world and to you. But gradually now, when I look at you, I see only swirling energy patterns, swirling in beautiful motions with everything else around you. I have to make a greater and greater effort of memory to visualize you as a singular notion of flesh and bone, because flesh and bone are purely concepts devised by the mind and the idea of separation. It's all garbage, actually!"

We guffawed with laughter that the human body and mind was all garbage!

"So truly, I am holding you back from your own development?"

"In your own mind only. Nothing is holding me back because I want what I have. I still want to see you and care for you, and provide a route for you to take away from grief and suffering and separation. Taking you to my world was partly designed to keep your attention away from your new girlfriend," she smiled. "But mostly because I wanted to bring you a new truth — a new purpose, and therefore help the world to acknowledge such a new purpose too. You see, I'm still in the physical world, though moving gradually away from it. And one other thing. I am not saying that God doesn't exist. I'm saying that God is everything. That you are God, this sofa is God, and as Mr. Salinger says in his book — all of a sudden I saw that she was God and the milk was God . . . all she was doing was pouring God into God . . . "

She became silent then, as though tired by this telling. For me, having a direct line to God was the most exciting thing I ever experienced, though the departure she kept mentioning left me with a stomachache.

But as I turned toward her again with another question, she smiled sheepishly and waved goodbye. Still, now I understood why she could not manage to stay with me all the time. She needed frequent breaks to rest from the garbage. So I woke up.

# NINE

And the beautiful gardens around the house continued to proliferate and grow richer. During the following days there was hardly a patch of my land without plant life. Everything blossomed and spread around me like a Garden of Eden without the troubles of evil and good, just good and beauty and life grew there with Nicki and I in residence. I imagined that she had imagined it all for our home between life and death.

The separation taking place between my soul and the world it inhabited grew now, and in some moments I began to experience actual pain, as though a resistance to this progress was still established, presumably because of my attachment to Gideon and his love.

It seemed strange to me that love could be a preventative to change, and I supposed that this was somewhat like the feelings the flesh produces in grief from the departed loved one. It is hard to stop the sadness that follows such loss. It's not possible to forget a deeply etched wound. It is only possible to love that which caused it.

As my evolution continued to unfold and reveal itself in all its magic, so the realizations popped up like ripe cherries ready to fall from the tree. My separation and my growing remoteness from Gideon and his corner of existence was not because I was loving him less, but because I was loving him more. The process whereby the lover becomes a saint in the mind of the grieving is perfectly natural, and offers the lover freedom from the wound caused by the loss. As I saw him further and further from me, so I saw him in his perfection. With my kiss upon his forehead I hoped to awaken his soul to the same potential. Thus we would walk among the trees and on the beach, all this from one kiss.

After the gathering of the three girls, Ansinoé and I continued to meet as lovers every so often, mostly in her home in Belvedere, where her cat Kadabra was the only one to complain. Carefully, Ansinoé did not try to replace Nicki. Nicki was still totally in residence in my life and we exchanged our love and thoughts daily.

The gardens about the Mill Valley house were so abundant that I could hardly believe my eyes each day. It was as though the trees and plants honored me by growing thicker and stronger and more frequently than anywhere else.

Ansinoé had come to the conclusion that I was getting younger by the day. I didn't discourage our meetings because the sex was so great, but eventually I had to bring some degree of truth to the situation. This was an affair for me, after all, not a total "marriage," for my love for Nicki still held me completely entranced. To my surprise, Ansinoé made no objection to this, but then our love affair was still very young, as was she.

Soon enough I began to believe in my own extended lifespan. Long hours of sleep ceased to be necessary, and when sleep came it was only a shallow replica of the old format. My "eyes," the eyes within my soul, were always open. I could see everything that was going on around me, even during sleep, except when I dreamed of Nicki and we walked and talked together, for then I entered a different reality. I never got the little sicknesses that others suffered — colds or flu or tiredness. There were no excuses for not living at the total full. My concentration on everything around me was greater. And that was the other thing. When would I die? In fifty years, even a hundred? The latter seemed slightly absurd and beyond my comprehension. How could anyone live that long? I felt a little freakish.

Sex was fabulous. It was so fabulous that I began to want it as much as I had in my twenties and thirties, back when I couldn't get enough. With Nicki, it was a kind of taunting, acceptably teasing reminder of those moments during childhood when the excitement of an event — a party, a gift, a specially loved item or moment — is so glorious that it somehow shines with light. It wasn't a fight or a conflict, and there was no peak or valley, but a kind of constant joyful deliverance.

"Incredible. Why didn't you do all this when I was in the body? We could have had such fun!" Nicki touched me intimately and I felt a tingle pass through my body. Lovemaking across the veil is a very special thing! Sometimes we would remain playing together on balmy Sunday mornings, but one particular Sunday I had invited Jennifer for lunch so I had to rise early and prepare for the event. Nicki was, for some reason best known to her, nervous about her arrival.

I was trying to make up for all the lack of attention I had shown Jennifer, and I hoped I'd have the chance to explain what had been happening. I was preparing a roast chicken and roast potatoes, a dish that afforded me the opportunity to drink gallons of wine before the meal.

She entered the kitchen and hugged me, then stopped dead in her tracks. Nicki was standing outside the sliding door onto the deck, and I could see her through the glass, looking even more like the apparition she was. It never occurred to me that Jennifer would see her too, but this time she did.

She became dizzy and fell back toward me as Nicki entered elegantly through the glass door, and stood right there in front of her.

"Oh, wow," I said. "You can see her."

"Yes, finally, Nicki, finally." I couldn't help laughing at this response and a big wide grin spread over Nicki's face.

"Why did you keep me waiting so long, Nick?"

"I'm sorry, Jennifer — I don't know. It wasn't me that kept you waiting."

"So the other side passes the buck just like this side, eh?" Jennifer was suddenly genuinely upset.

"So it seems. I had to do things with Gideon first. I didn't choose this delay. I don't have control any more than you do."

"Oh, God, and after all this time I can't even hug you." Jennifer fussed.

"Yes, you can. Come closer — it works."

They hugged in their way, and I watched Jennifer flush from the experience.

"But you saw me before, at the Depot café, remember?" Nicki stood back now and looked at Jennifer, her neglected life-long friend.

"Yes, but I didn't believe that — it was too unreal, too weird then."

"And now it's real?"

"Yes. Now it's really real. So good to see you, even as a ghost."

"So how has all this been for you?" Nicki sat in the chair normally occupied by Tashy during our breakfasts together. Tashy appeared and jumped to the nearby window ledge, staring at Nicki's image, entirely unfazed by it all.

"Are you crazy? How has it been? Completely incredible. I knew it was real, all this talk about you coming back. But somehow the knowledge of it doesn't really overcome the doubts. I felt you. I knew you hadn't left us, but I couldn't believe it because, well, who does? Gideon was showing signs of premature dementia, but then there's all that stuff about his aging retardation and the way he was behaving as though he was entirely happy with everything. How could he be happy after you'd gone, unless you hadn't?"

I saw them smile together as they had years before, doubtless even before Nicki and I became lovers. They were together again and I figured it might work better if I took my leave.

Jennifer had no interest in the meal I had prepared, so I left her with Nicki to catch up and fell asleep on the living room sofa. This was the first time that Nicki had actually appeared to anyone other than me, and this knowledge greatly dignified my place in the valley of the dead. Nicki's ghost had to be real, unless of course Jennifer was as crazy as I was and we were both suffering from some drunken illusion of the afterlife.

I woke in the middle of that night shouting and groaning. There was some kind of pressure and strain in the back of my head recently, now more intense than usual.

Nicki was not there, and Jennifer had evidently left, so I slept again and in that second sleep I dreamed that Nicki and Jennifer sat together on the beach near the forest and beckoned to me to sit with them. Nicki and I sandwiched Jennifer between our bodies, holding her with immense love and rocking back and forth with Jennifer's head on Nicki's shoulder.

The sacred shows no signs of development, nothing other than absolute presence. Thought cannot encompass it nor understand it, for thought is one step behind its truth. This special mystical state happens instantly, and although thought may follow it, it has no value, for the instant nature of this sacred state is known — is a fact and outside space and time — immediate and entirely in the present moment.

After dreaming of Jennifer and Nicki, I was wakeful again but calmer, and I felt the presence of perfect, simple beauty, without comment or pleasure and pain — just the moment of absolute oneness with life itself. It was a benediction that flooded in through the window and occupied me, held me in its power, raising me up, and then departing in its own time never to return in that exact form. The body was no more than the vessel, functioning, empty, still and absolute. For the first time and the last I was in bliss. I knew in that moment, however long it lasted, where Nicki was in her land where spirits rest.

# TEN

"I'm growing tired," Nicki said to me one day as we walked together.

"Tired?" I felt a pang of alarm strike through my chest. "Tired of me?"

"Silly, no, just somehow exhausted, you know, like when you don't sleep properly for a few nights and everything just feels a bit deflated."

"Do you ever sleep?" I stopped and touched her arm.

"No, well, kind of — hibernation would be a better word."

"In that place where you guys all go to rest?" My old instincts, born from my relationship with my mother, made me want to lift Nicki from her sadness through humor.

"Yes." She didn't bite. "Don't worry. It will probably pass."

How can you fill words with a life? It's like trying to draw a picture of fire burning. How can I bring the character, the foibles, and the truth of Nicki to a ghost and then express them in any authentic way to offer up who she is? I am at a loss to do so. I am inadequate beyond the attempt, for her body has gone, and even if it were not gone I would be straining like an empty goblet eager to be drunk. And encountering the spirit world was an added complication. She would lead me to the trees that she told me were the portals to her world, though her answers to my eager questions were as vague and mysterious as her apparent life — be it life.

Nicki lectured me during those days on the infinite compassion of the universe, what she called the human "uncertainty principle." Only humans were uncertain and everything else knows the answers. This, she told me, was the only reason why we suffer so much and nothing else does! Made sense, especially spoken with that wry smile she had developed since her "enlightenment."

It had taken me quite a while to get over her growing independence from me. I could no longer corner her with emotional bribes or attract her with hormonal enticements, threats, victimizations, or vibrations. She wasn't susceptible any more to my tricks and devices, though she was still entirely loving and attentive. And as I gave up the ideas of entrapping her, our friendship and love affair took on a new form. We were free from each other, and so our love for each other was unencumbered and thenceforth everlasting.

But this did not end the story of the kiss she had planted on my frantic brow. Still the butterfly flapped its wings and changed my temperate state.

Still Mother Earth had not completed Her pattern for those of us who noticed. I had understood at last what Nicki had meant by my stepping on the butterfly — that the stopping of the earthquake had been our act of power. We had together influenced life, and all that followed the kiss was a consequence of it — my slower aging, the fecundity of nature about my home, the realizations that kept coming. She called it clumsy in her humorous way, but actually it was a giant and significant presence of a real god in my life.

During the late spring of that year, Nicki and I decided to take a vacation in Italy. Strange though it may seem, we could envisage being together in another place, even another country. It was an attempt on my part to keep her with me for longer, as she seemed to be drifting behind that absorbing veil.

"How shall we go, by car or magic carpet?" I asked her, with a growing flutter in my heart.

"Let's find each other's way. You take a flight, and I'll watch over the airplane. I'll go by soulscape and you can search the skies for my arrival. I've never been to Tuscany. Is it beautiful?"

"More beautiful than your resting paradise — too beautiful for humans, but just right for Italians."

I chose Tuscany as the location, intending that we might walk together in those loving Italian hills. Now that I had so much time and space to occupy me for the rest of my long life, so there was that dread thing called leisure. I'd decided to take a sabbatical from Berkeley to allow any remaining gossip to die naturally, and in any case, these bizarre days, I didn't really care if anybody noticed or not.

Jennifer worried and promised a visit, and Ansinoé promised not to, seeming to understand more than I did what the purpose of this spiritual vacation was to be.

That glorious Tuscan house rested across the bosom of a hill, entered through an army of cypresses along a rough-stone path. And so close to Florence, so close to Dante and Beatrice, doorway to the underworld, which lay beneath our heaven.

The villa I rented stood just outside the village of Falciani, thirty minutes from Florence. It was a small community of some twenty astonishingly beautiful homes, completely invisible to any tourist visitor, and more important, away from prying eyes. I soon developed again my addiction for Tuscany and now for the house, set in thirty acres of land, mostly forest, with its own home-grown wild boar and porcupine in the woods, peacocks in the fields, and pheasants fluttering and screeching at the bottom of the wild garden.

I knew the very first moment I walked through the broad front gate that there was something unique about this villa, and that some miracle would occur there. It had that similarity of atmosphere, like an ancient church, of inlaid holiness, but imbued also in this case with a certain mischief, as though an enigmatic ghost were present. I assumed this was Nicki, for she appeared fairly quickly after I set up shop.

"New home?" she asked.

"For a while," I said. "We have some talking to do, I think."

"Yes, and all the time in the world to do it." She floated away with that enigmatic comment, and left me to appraise our meeting place.

Standing before the entrance I felt a soft breeze slip through my hair and take shape behind me, almost as though a gentle hand were caressing the back of my head. I turned to see nothing but the magnificent hills and valleys of this Tuscan heaven. There was an unevenness about everything — the shape of the house, the slope of the lawn at the front. The trees themselves seemed almost to be leaning in an odd direction, as though not quite obeying the laws of nature.

The contrasts in Tuscany are blazing hot summer and Arctic winter, iron and gold, tired and passionate, deep day and lightning-night. The spring is awakening, the fall poetic; there is silence in the very air of the mornings.

I remember the certain dewiness in the air, an early-morning shiver of unfamiliarity. My imagined pleasure at coming to a new location and taking delight in the glory of Italy was tempered by uncertainty, as though the house had a mind to overcome my joy with doubt in unwelcome. All this could be attributed to the uncertainty of Nicki's continuing presence in my life, and somehow the villa gave me further unreason to believe there was an extra "catch" — another dénouement to encounter before it was all concluded.

Once again I found Gideon's place in the physical world while he found mine in the ethereal. I knew also that this trip was his way of saying sorry for making me jealous — so he thought I was — and to help secure our love affair from further stretching. I had never been to Tuscany in my life, and now, odd to relate, I was going to be there in my death. In contemplation it all seems utterly unbelievable, but for me it was very simple. I just imagined the place and found myself there even before Gideon landed from the local airport.

"So, you just arrive? Just like that?" He smiled at me.

"Yes — by Spirit Air. Don't you just love it?"

The atmosphere of Tuscany is in the air itself. Once there, standing amongst the cypresses that filled the driveway and the gardens, I just felt like giggling and lying on my back in the deep grass, looking up at the tops of the trees and the sky. I felt reborn as I stepped through the rich and lavish undergrowth, with endless tingles of warmth and glory from my Mother still, the Earth.

❦

That first balmy morning, as I unpacked the car into the villa, there was the sound of dogs barking in the distance and a power saw working somewhere. Sound carried far through those hills, leaving a loneliness and despair that would be banished by the unfolding day. It felt good always to stand outside the entrance to the villa. I knew that no one would greet me, and the neighbors were about their own business, unconcerned with my daily life.

"Who built this place?" Nicki asked, on the first of our walks around the property.

"An Italian duke — Mark Antonio Catalana-Gonzaga — Italian royalty. His family leased it to the Vatican, probably St. Peter himself. It's well over a thousand years old."

"You love this country, don't you?" Her body faded as the sun shone from behind her, and I worried that it would burn her soul and she would vanish again.

"More than anywhere in the world. I first came here about ten years before we met and fell in love with it all, especially Florence. I vowed to die here actually."

"My God, you mean there was a time before we met? I can't imagine that now."

"There'll be a time after we depart too, I guess." I fished.

167

"And the villa? What's it called? 'La Docciola?'"

"Yes, though it doesn't really mean anything in English. Maybe, 'the sweetness.'"

The immediate garden was beautiful, often enhanced by a slim black cat which appeared almost every time we walked, and perched on the top of the narrow fencing that separated one part of the land from fields beyond. She would stare at us cautiously for a moment and then avert her eyes in that casual, disinterested way cats do, even when they see ghosts.

"Cats always see you."

"And dogs, but dogs are too shy and silly to be obvious!"

"Can you read their thoughts too?"

"They don't have thoughts, only pictures and emotions. They feel everything much faster than we do. Everything for animals is about awareness. Watch a cat's eyes and see how she responds to every little nuance of life around her. I think I'd like to be a cat, but I doubt that option's available now."

"Do you have options?" I tried again to get some sort of guidance from her.

"Not really, and even if I did I doubt they would be visible to me until one of them was about to be chosen on my behalf."

"Who by?"

"God knows, I guess." She smiled and moved closer to me. "Don't be so serious — everything will be okay." I did not believe her.

The grass had been recently mown but there was already a scattering of pinecones fallen in the healthy winds that gust everywhere in Tuscany at that time of year. At the very back of the villa were two large sets of double doors, one that entered the house, with green, slatted shutters, locked and barred. The other set was lower down in the belly of the house, and much larger. The gardener referred to it as a "cantina," and told me that it contained old wine vats and broken furniture which was used to replace worn window frames and doors.

Down the bottom of the garden, a large gate gave way to the forest, and as I stood looking into the thick wooded foliage, I could hear the sound of snuffling boars that seemed to frighten off the birds.

"But something is happening right? I mean, you're different, more loving in a way, but also more distant."

"Yes, something is happening, something very fundamental, but I have no real idea what it is. I just know that it's right and we have no choice but to let it develop. This is an ideal place for it too. Your instincts are always right, Gideon, always." We were silent then, just walking and feeling that extraordinary landscape and listening to nature. I fell into her softness and gave up my fears for a while, but before long I felt those pangs of doubt again.

"I wish I could understand. I feel powerless somehow, my heart fluttering every time I see you now. I guess it's been like that from the beginning, since you died, as though I have no control over my own life because I'm so attached to you. But now I feel it more because we're no longer really attached and there's nothing I can do about it."

"I know, and I feel it too, a sort of inevitability that neither of us can stop."

"Why can't we stop it? Why can't we simply call a halt and say we'll remain here like this forever."

"Because there is no forever."

It suddenly felt cold outside, and my heart froze over with her words. We walked back into the villa to try to find some warmth again.

Inside, the villa was classically beautiful, with too many rooms for a man and a ghost. Directly opposite the front entrance hung a seventeenth-century banner with faded colors and rotting stitching, draped from an old wooden pole and covering the door to a small bathroom. To the left were heavy stone steps down to the kitchen, where the table was too big to move and the cooker seemingly as old as the house. Huge empty basket-covered wine vats lined one wall, beneath a massive sink with its plumbing guts hanging loose like a cow's udder. A door led out into the garden from there also, and the floor was stone cold, old, and worn without a touch of welcome. We would begin our days here, Nicki watching me drink pints of Italian coffee, plus fresh bread and croissants delivered by the local café.

"Why didn't we ever come here before, when I was alive?" We sat in the kitchen together the following morning.

"Good question. Why didn't we do all sorts of things before, when you were alive?"

"Well, I guess that's only regret. Why would we regret? We're here now after all. Wish I could drink some of that coffee, though."

"One good reason to remain alive." We were still intermittently silent that morning especially, as though there were important things brewing. I kept wanting to persuade her, in my foolish hanging-on, to not declare anything that would be an ending, my mind constantly searching for ways to manipulate life the way I wished it to be.

"It's almost as though we were still alive together. I can even imagine it. Can't you make this so, Nicki? Can't you bring yourself back to life? It would be such fun just to spend a few weeks sampling the Tuscan sun."

She smiled at me, and I could see her tears as they gently shed down her cheeks. I felt so bad at making her cry, and I couldn't even grasp her body and comfort her. I couldn't take her in my arms and tell her it was going to be okay because I knew it wasn't and anyway, she wasn't really there, after all.

The upper floor was enormous, with a long corridor running from one end to the other with seven bedrooms leading off on either side. The first main

171

bedroom was set against the corner of the house where the morning sun flooded in on both sides, banishing any sense of uncertainty. This was the room we spent our nights together in, waking to that everlasting sun.

We felt small there and alone, a good feeling in a way, for we could indulge our appetite for one another's talk sitting on the bed. I forgot my fantasies, my fears, sometimes, and then we were happy. We had found another haven. Jennifer never came for her visit, leaving us in this human paradise, the resting place for living souls.

You know how lovers talk when they're first together, and how that talk becomes consumed by all the strivings of everyday life? We create the love affair and then forget about it in preference to the engineering of its support — homes, children, loans, increased desires. We start by flying and then pummel ourselves with engines to keep us in the air — and so the engines weigh us down until the ground leaps up to break our wings. If it were ever possible to be reborn as lovers, Gideon and I found how to do it in Tuscany, within that glorious house and its surrounding lands. We talked and walked all the time.

Our day began early. In the service of the ancient window shutters of Italy, light isn't really excluded but tempered. For a time, my clarity of existence increased.

"I can see you better today," he said. "You're not so invisible. What happened?"

"Strange, huh? I do feel more visible somehow, but I'm not entirely sure that it's for reasons either of use would want to hear."

"Oh, dear. Are you about to devastate me again?" He paled slightly.

"Is that what I do, devastate you?" We sat down on the grass and he grabbed one of the fallen pinecones to occupy his hands.

"Yes, but you did that when you were alive too," he said.

"Is that bad?"

"Bad? Depends on whether you want a peaceful life or not. Life with you wasn't peaceful, I suppose, though that never reduced my love for you."

"And now?" I watched his face.

"You're a mover, Nicki, a shaker, not a peacemaker, not for me anyway." He threw the pinecone as though to emphasize his resentment.

"Are you angry with me?"

"I never really understood your love for me. I could never fathom it — not just why you loved me — this is just lack of self-regard — but *how* you loved me. It always seemed to me such a mystery, I guess, as you were also a mystery to me. I never could figure you out — how you would behave next — how you loved me. And now I can't figure out how you can be going,

173

why you have to go. Why can't life and death be one, as you say they are?"

"Oh, that's a lot of questions." I faded slightly, losing my confidence at his demands.

"Not questions, just uncertainties. You don't have to answer me. You don't have to be the diviner and the oracle all the time." He grabbed another pinecone and ducked his head sideways out of the direct rays of the sun so as to see my expression. "Don't you in your wisdom see what this is for me? I love you so much that I cannot stop your progress away from me. It would be like trying to prevent God from making his plans."

"And you have your own life too," I ventured, unsure of how much we were going to delve into this most sensitive of matters.

He sputtered and coughed in that characteristic manner displaying disapproval. It was tough for him, for during our lives together he had been many years my senior, more wise, more understanding. He had often mentored me and therefore tolerated my immaturity. Yet all this had changed since I had left my body, as though in death I had suddenly become many decades more able, my words, and actions, somehow singing the songs of elders.

"Yes, I have my own life, a life that you have departed from once already, and now it seems you plan to do it again." Once more a pinecone darted across the deep lawn.

"I plan nothing. It just seems to be happening. Anyway, who says it's what you fear? How do you know I'm leaving you? Where do you get your ideas? Maybe you're wrong."

"There's so much more to say and do yet, isn't there?" He struggled against tears, the sadness beginning to burst through his defenses.

"Coming to terms in relationships is always about a contract with roses and thorns. It'll be okay, I promise it'll be okay."

"Really?" His face lit up and he smiled again, thank God. I loved it when he smiled and his eyes turned from gray to blue.

As my presence increased in that ancient land, so also came the increase in my energy. We touched more; we even managed more of our particular variety of lovemaking where I brought such stimulation to his body that he exploded in my absent hands — as he told me, "unlike any time during our living lives together." I managed to bring a physical fulfillment to him that was new and fresh.

When the full mornings brought us out of the villa gardens, our walks amidst the bright green and yellow hills often took us to the local town, San Casciano in Val Di Pesa — Macchiavelli's birthplace. A mile or so from the house, the two-thousand-year-old streets were filled with tiny stores bursting with fresh salad and vegetables, big-bellied fathers and intolerant mothers — children scampering about in confusion beneath their feet. Gideon was welcomed by everyone — no matter his poor Italian — and some of the older women even "saw" me beside him, their seasoned eyes willing to accept the ghosts of nature. Gideon was popular with the mothers, for he loved children. There were moments in my heart when I wished that I could have left him with a child, but then, had there been a child I would not have left, sickness or no sickness.

"Change keeps forcing us to let go. It's not that we want to let go — we never do, but somehow it has to happen despite our attempts to stop it. We barter with existence and it listens to our prayers, and is kind to us much of the time, but it moves on nevertheless."

"So you're not going to be with me forever, is that what you're saying?" He pledged, still, that endless human failing, the need to remain.

"I can't say that. I don't know that. I don't know anything truly, except that I must do what I am bidden, whatever that may be. I could tell you to bring about your own death, but how violent that would be. You might end up with me in some form, but who knows where you would have to go and whether we would be together? All that is foolish conjecture."

"Okay, okay. I can't argue against truth, but it's your truth. I just want to keep on seeing you and knowing you forever."

Then we returned to the garden that day, that sunny, full-bodied Italian afternoon and held each other in that awesome knowledge of inevitability.

"I can tell you," he said at last, "one thing is for sure. I will never know this again. I will never be so sure as I am now of the purity and godliness of love in this form. This you have brought me, and nothing can ever replace it." And still we held one another, and still we cried.

❧

One night, a sudden thunderclap brought rain in torrents. The air cleared, the birds got up off their backs, the animals climbed the cedars in the garden, and the neighbor's dog barked at the lightning and ran under the house. In the early morning hours I put on my night shirt in holy celebration, a sort of existential worship of the spring equinox. Nicki and I clasped one another and felt that eternal energy passed between us as love, resting thereafter from what seemed a lifetime's abstinence.

We had no sour moments, no angry days, for we knew somewhere in our hearts that this was an ending, some kind of transformation that would alter our togetherness and change it into a new story.

The skies changed suddenly again after the storm. Sparkling shadows dowsed the earth, defining the sunrise. Long grey-green frosts melted into steam above the grass, and the birds flew faster against the

177

cold. The mornings were so still I thought of frozen lakes, and frozen dreams. What could anything do to hurt me, truly? She had told me we would always be together. Did she lie, or was there a greater authority of which even she was ignorant?

Perhaps it would never end, I thought, but one day Nicki wasn't there in the morning when I woke. The sharp shadows of falling light were not interrupted by her glancing presence. I walked about the gardens uselessly, in a state of fear and doubt greater than when she first died. I tussled with my conscience, questioned all that I had not done to make her spirit rest and stay with me forever, until I ended, sitting on the doorstep stroking the cat that lived in the fields. But she returned as though nothing had happened.

"Have you come back for good?" I asked.

"I don't know."

"I've locked myself out, I was so distressed."

"It's time to go home." She sort-of-smiled.

"Hm." I watched the cat's eyes looking from one to the other of us.

# ELEVEN

Marin County was ever glorious, and the garden at home had grown even more colorful with Jennifer attending as well as she could, adopted by Tashy but abandoned by the other cats, who had taken up temporary residence with various spoiling neighbors. But they returned a day after my arrival, treating me badly for a few days thereafter.

Ansinoé looked pale and beautiful, her long black hair still longer, cascading about her shoulders like a river flowing over her body. Unlike Jennifer, she had not encountered Nicki in person, but she tried to tell me that there was no need for it. I figured that if Nicki wanted it, it would happen. Ansinoé was cool at first. After all, I had spent time away with my ghostly wife, and she must have wondered what kind of partner I might make. But our affair was young, as she was, and she seemed willing to wait.

The tender connection between us took up its pace a few nights after my home coming and, for a while Nicki was absent. I wondered if she had decided to haunt the Italian villa for a while longer — was this how things worked in the afterlife? I could imagine that ghosts might be happiest in those ancient lands.

It seemed so strange to me, as I watched the lovers in the turmoil of sexual love, wasting their time on fripperies and performances — why did they not know what this was all about? Even Gideon had no notion of what was happening to him. I had, after all, taken him to my own world, my own home, and shown him my fantasies; shown him his power — the power of the kiss. Yet still he continued in confusion.

I, of course, knew it all! I was the perpetrator, and the miracle-maker. I knew their hearts and souls, these humans of the flesh. What more therefore could I be in this story but a critic?

How depressing. Here I was the watchful witness, hating it, penetrating it as they penetrated one another. Here was I watching the final dénouement without knowing what the hell it was, believing in my own enlightenment and entirely mistaken. Here I was — here I wasn't. I had thought, in my spirit fantasy, that I was on the upward trail, rising from the human to the spirit and enlightenment. How was I to know that all roads lead home again?

But it was also good to see the two of them in a tender love affair. She attended to him like a slave to a god, and although I disapproved of her approach, I enjoyed seeing him spoiled to pieces. Gideon — my love, my storm of events — relished her visits to our bed, like a child with a new toy. He had nothing to lose — truly nothing.

And as I referenced life through observations of his progress, I ignored the truth of my place in it. Where was I in all this, once again? Why was I still here? Why had I imagined myself enlightened? Thus existence and my death drew me back to the three basic questions of the immortal spirit — who am I, where do I come from, and where am I going? I did not, still, know the answer to any of these questions, so what enlightenment was here?

I found myself looking at Ansinoé one night as she slept beside him. She had accepted that I was a presence in Gideon's life without so much of a complaint, though she "saw" me only through his vision and must often have thought the whole thing entirely strange. What woman is willing to tolerate an ex-lover in their bed, let alone the ghost of one? It might have become something of a soap opera had it not changed. In those next days, Gideon's concentration on her during my apparent absence gave me the opportunity to see him alone, and alone he quickly turned for comfort to another. This was to be expected. This was natural enough — love is so vital to the living spirit.

While I sat there trying to figure them out she woke, and sat at the end of the bed, evidently not aware of me.

She was quite naked, and I watched her beautiful body, slight but full and rounded, her shoulders narrow, her breasts handsomely large, the stomach a little rounded, her whole body so sweet I could have remained there watching her for hours. She brushed her hair, singing almost in a whisper, and I could hear her thoughts, though I did not wish her to hear mine. I did not want her to see me, so I sat there — a ghostly Peeping Tom, quite unashamed, quite silent, holding my breath, doing to her exactly what I had done to Gideon in our first days after my death.

As I watched, I noticed that there was a different atmosphere about the house, about the room, the air, outside. The feeling was eerie, ghostly, I guess, except that there was no fear in it for me, only curiosity. I had the feeling that we were not at my old home anymore but in some alien place.

Ansinoé turned toward me and smiled but the smile was not for me, for her eyes were directed slightly to one side and unfocused. The smile was for herself, into a mirror that hung behind me in her world. She tilted her head and continued brushing. She stopped and moved back to the top of the bed. She climbed under the covers again next to Gideon. He made no movement, even though she leaned over him and watched his breathing briefly. She loved him, I saw, and I only feared it a little now.

I sat there, my chin in my palm, gazing at her face as she lay only a few feet away quite unaware of me.

She turned out the light beside the bed. All I could see now were vague shapes and clean white sheets and pillows.

In the early morning light I followed her as she left the room for the library next door. I waited for a moment, for I truly did have another purpose other than pure voyeurism! There was something increasingly odd about the rooms, about the feeling of the house. The bedroom in which Gideon lay sleeping felt larger, as though I was in the midst of a childhood nightmare where everything seems to recede, where the brain does tricks with the eyes and sends pictures on the walls off into the distance. But as she disappeared into the library, this feeling vanished. Perhaps this was merely the change of environment since our return from the Italian villa, or perhaps something in me was changing yet again.

I waited. Everything felt almost normal, but still I knew something significant had happened here in the home that had been mine for so long.

I could not, would not appear to her. What was the point? So I departed in my sponsored way. I was the spirit, after all. I could win over the living. I finally realized what all this was about. Poor Ansinoé — all she had was a human child to give birth to, just conceived that night in her womb. In this sarcasm I felt the deepest depression, deeper even than realizing my death. But it was laced with something far greater

and far more frightening than death — it was laced
with life.

⁂

"Can we go and see a psychic?" Ansinoé burst into
the room suddenly. It was morning, and I had been
in a deep sleep, dreaming again of Nicki. She had
been telling me something, though on waking I could
not remember it, and I felt vaguely irritated with
Ansinoé for cutting short one of my nightly visits with
Nicki. Ansinoé looked radiant and frightened all at
the same time.

"Of course — why not? There are bound to be
plenty round here. Are you okay?" She slipped into
bed and nuzzled up against me. Here, I realized, was
my new lover — living and warm beside me.

I called and managed to find a famous lady in
San Francisco called Vera Chiesa who quickly made
time for us, as though she'd been expecting us. Her
eagerness suggested that we were important, but then
I imagined she spoke like that to all her clients —
never lose a sale in America. Nicki didn't appear that
day, or the next, as Ansinoé and I set off in the car to
the city.

Ansinoé was mostly silent, and I asked her several
times if she was all right. She smiled and nodded that
she was, until eventually she got fed up with hearing
the question and told me to shut up. So we drove over
the Golden Gate in silence.

Vera Chiesa was no more than five feet tall, so tiny in size that only when I sat down near her did we see eye to eye. Her power and presence, however, was bigger than both of us, and she puffed continuously on a joint which she gripped between her two middle fingers and drew the smoke from the hole made by her clenched fist.

She spoke very quickly, but we made a tape recording of the whole session that lasted no more than five minutes.

"Your child will bring back new life that will help the dead one to depart. Your life, sweet mother, will find great joy in this match and this child, for you are the greatest of women, and the best of lovers and mothers.

"You, old father of all this work, can never lose the heart and soul that continued to love you even after death, for the kiss she planted grows into a butterfly that unfolds its wings before you. Take great care, man. There is much to be done from your heart's forge, for this forge was born from an angel who even comes back as spirit for you — though not only for you — for herself also."

She ended this extraordinary soliloquy as abruptly as she had begun it, took a huge puff on her joint, smiled at us both and left the room as though nothing at all significant had been said, leaving no time or space for questions. Ansinoé and I sat there, open-mouthed, and then we trudged out of the room, down the stairs and into the street trying to digest what had happened. At least, I was trying to digest what had happened. It seemed that Ansinoé already had.

"Did you get all that? Are you pregnant?" I asked as I helped her into the car.

"Yes — I knew it already." She smiled that beatific smile.

"How? When?" I almost yelled this.

"She was in the house last night."

"My God, you mean Nicki came? Why didn't you tell me last night? I mean, why didn't you tell me you were pregnant? I mean both — you know."

"Because then I didn't know, and neither did she."

"Did you see her?"

"No, but I felt her there, watching me."

"So you believe it?"

"Of course I believe it. It's perfectly obvious, isn't it?"

I started the car up and pulled out, suddenly thinking I had to be very careful now — even more careful. I drove very slowly!

But did this mean that my Nicki was finally gone? Hadn't she promised me that she'd be with me forever, always by my side?

"She will be with you," Ansinoé answered my thoughts. "She'll be with you forever, in many forms, who knows?"

"Do you believe all that stuff? I mean, this Vera Chiesa, she's just a local psychic. What does she know?"

"She seemed to know quite a bit, actually."

"Yes, but they pick things up from you when you're sitting there. They see inside you somehow. And they always phrase things ambiguously, leaving the rest to your imagination." I wondered at myself, the phenomenologist, the ghost-hunter — couldn't even believe in a psychic!

"Thus spake the man with a living ghost." We laughed. "I think it's wonderful. I'm going to have a baby."

Was it wonderful? What about my lover Nicki? What about my wise and wonderful wife, Nicki? I felt like crying.

The onrush of existence shocked me, for it was as I left Ansinoé that I "got it" so to speak. I knew in that moment also that I would not be given any time to consider the decision that had been made. There was barely a chance even to ask the questions, "Who's making the decision?" "Where was I going? I was having fun right where I was!" But there were no answers except one — it was time for me to move on.

Nothing is self-indulgent in life — somehow completely banishing any idea of God in all this. *Life happens,* as they say on bumper stickers. And what happens, happens completely — the change of state from life to death and then the change of state beyond death — all perfectly natural and smooth — except that few, if any, get the opportunity to see it all as I was. Or perhaps I was wrong even in that. Perhaps all spirits saw as I saw, each on their own level of existence, each finding their own truth.

And where was my Gideon in all this? I had left him in some way once Ansinoé appeared on the scene, but I still longed to see him, still loved to walk with him and advise him each day. It felt so replete, so uncomplicated. But of course life is not uncomplicated for long. There has always to be something new to contend with, and this was my new condition — to move on beyond the veil to something other than his wife.

Nature should bring us out of the possessiveness and sexuality of the lover more easily, so that we can become something different more easily. Different? Yes, different, but all knowledge of it obliterated by a new birth.

In my last act of watching Gideon from my place beside the veil I saw him spread the remainder of my ashes in the garden outside the house.

I stood beside him and touched his arm, but at first he did not sense my presence.

"Oh, God," he said. "It's like the first time. It's like I never saw you before. What shall I do, Nicki? Can't I die right here and now and drift away with you? Why does it have to hurt so much?"

"It won't hurt for long. Let it all pass. Remember, please, God, remember what you said." I clutched at his arm, intertwined my energy into his for that final moment, so painful.

*"One thing is for certain. I will never know this again. I will never be so sure as I am now of the purity and godliness of love in this form. This you have brought me, and nothing can ever replace it."*

And still we held one another, and still we cried, heart-to-heart, soul-to-soul.

California, April 2003

# Acknowledgments

Love and thanks to Manuela, who gave birth to this book, to Jackie Joiner for her vital early input, to Roy M. Carlisle for being the best of editors, to Dorian Gossy for the work that hurt, to Kristen Garneau for the title she gave so generously, to Beth Moon for her fabulous photograph entitled "Church Yews" which forms the basis for the cover art, to Yatri, the man with the light and my greatest friend, and to Priya as always, for making the space in my life that allowed me to do it at all.

# About the Author

Philip Dunn is a book creator with some three hundred book titles to his credit, and also the author of some thirty volumes of non-fiction. He lives in California and is currently working on several new books, including a new novel.